WALK LIKE A MAN

WALK LIKE A MAN

by
Donald Honig

WILLIAM SLOANE ASSOCIATES

New York

Copyright © 1961 by Donald Honig
All rights reserved.
Published simultaneously in the Dominion of
Canada by George J. McLeod Limited, Toronto.
Printed in the United States of America.

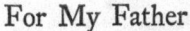

PART ONE

CHAPTER 1

1

The three of us, Rachel and Tom and myself, were crouched before the loft's small window watching; although Tom was hardly able to see, and he was sitting behind watching us more than the window. Rachel's face was closest to the window and once I looked at her and knew I would never forget how she looked then, her horror and vague fascination; her face looked like marble, a hard, fixed stare in her eyes, not looking like a woman (or a living woman anyway), even though she was just eighteen and very beautiful with long, yellow hair that swept back over her shoulders.

The men were down in the yard, at least twenty of them, sullen and grim, hard and expectant with the imminence of achievement as if they had been waiting all their lives for this (and probably some of them had, for not many of the men in Capstone had ever liked Uncle Clay, had hated him in fact, because he was always quicker than any of them, on his feet and on a horse and with a pistol and in his thinking as well: always quicker, faster, sharper), and they reminded me of iron, they were like that, like my impression of iron: brutal, unshakeable, bloodless. They looked quite dark in the fading light, like a mob of men crowded together will, their bearded faces dark and tyrannical, and behind them their horses standing like lectured beasts with hung heads and obedient immobility, some of the horses standing under the tree, dwarfed by it (as everything else seemed dwarfed by that tree—the house and the barn and all the other trees and even time). Most of the men had rifles, others pistols, and they all were showing them except the two that were pushing Uncle Clay toward the tree. Uncle Clay was walking so tall and straight and so slow that it didn't seem as though he was going to die in a few moments. He was bareheaded and he looked very thin without his coat, his legs like saplings with his breeches tucked tightly into the boots he told me he had taken from a Confederate officer he had killed.

They're going to try to hang Uncle Clay, I thought, and I was fascinated, almost as if I wanted to see it happen, because it was impossible; because it was Uncle Clay, who had fought duels in South Carolina before the war, who had taught me to ride and to use a pistol, and who had made Rachel cry the last time he had gone away, and who had made her cry again when he came back last night. But now she wasn't crying, just watching with that cold visionary look of someone expecting to see a miracle that would end all of life with a single blow; just watching, unalarmed as yet because she probably sensed as I did that they would not be able to hang him, that in a moment he would turn on them and laugh and fight free of them and ride off.

We could see, by leaning forward a bit, where Pa lay,

where he had fought the three of them as the others were dragging Uncle Clay from the house; and where now one of them was keeping him down with the pitchfork on his chest, the man's elbow jutting out at an angle as if he would drive the pitchfork right through Pa if Pa tried to get up. Another man was standing near them and we could hear this one saying, "Don't try to stop it, Adam. We're going to do it and you can't stop us." And every time Pa moved his hands the jutting elbow would stiffen with a thrust, and Pa's hands would shut into helpless raging fists and fall away.

Adamson had the rope. He was walking behind Uncle Clay, smaller than Uncle Clay, grim and dogged and implacable. They were almost to the tree. And then I knew that it was going to happen. Not because of the twenty men or because of the rope or because Pa couldn't stop it; not any of that: because of the tree. The tree was going to do it, let it be done. It towered over everything as if casting dark benedictions, having risen and shot from a mighty twisted trunk, like another world with its hundreds of boughs and twigs and its myriad dark, jungled, intricate leaves. Because Uncle Clay had crossed its roots and passed into its shadows, the thick underlimbs just above his head now in thrusting suspension; into the realm of the great maple that for hundreds of years had been lifting its limbs and shedding its leaves and absorbing the shadows of men.

And then Uncle Clay must have known, realized it too. He began to squirm and then to struggle. Two of the men grabbed him and tried to tie his wrists behind him. Now he was fighting. A few minutes ago I would have said *Now. He's going to get away now.* But I knew it wasn't going to happen. He was fighting in desperation, in terror, twisting about, throwing his arms at the men who had begun to surge around, animated by his sudden struggling. I leaned forward, biting my lip. Uncle Clay was going to die. I had known it before he did, and now he knew too. The men were saying things now, closing in on him, making him smaller as they grew larger. Then he fell down. I could see him through the legs of the men, scratching and twisting on the ground. They hauled him to his feet, mobbing around him, and we saw his face for a moment, contorted, broken-looking and not like Uncle Clay's face at all. They were dragging him nearer the tree and we saw the rope suddenly float up and fall, looping the branch and now Uncle Clay was really fighting, kicking and ducking as they raised the noose before him. One grabbed his hair from behind and jerked up his head and we saw his throat come taut and his white teeth suddenly appear naked and grimacing and he started to kick and twist and heave his shoulders as they tried to work the noose onto him.

And then Rachel cried, "Why is he doing that!" Her eyes were almost furious, almost tragic with disbelief.

I looked at her, amazed. "Do you think he wants to die?" I said.

2

I had just finished with the cows the evening before and was coming out of the barn when I saw Uncle Clay galloping up the road. It was just after dusk and he looked very small and fast coming up the road, crouched forward over the horse's shoulders like he was in a race, and once, just as he came into the yard, he did look back to see if anyone was near him. The way he looked back, so quick and sharp and intent, made me look down the road too. But no one was there. Then he was in the yard and his sorrel had galloped to a halt and he had dismounted and was walking quickly toward the house, his hat in his hand now, his pistols rattling against his legs. I stood in the barn doorway and watched him and he didn't see me and I didn't say anything. I watched him pass under the tree and pass the well and go up onto the porch, walking with the same hard intent quickness with which he had ridden, tall and erect, but harassed now, in a way I had never seen him before; and even though I had not seen him for months I remembered the way he had looked before, the way he had always looked, and this was not it and the first thing I thought was that something had gone bad in the war and that he had come to tell Pa about it.

Then he was through the door and into the house. I looked again down the road, into the gray motionless summer darkening; it seemed to bode something, there was too much stillness, the kind of mysterious interminable stillness that can gather for day upon day in the summer.

Then I was walking across the yard too, hurrying because I knew that Uncle Clay never stayed very long and I wanted to have every minute with him that I possibly could. When I entered the house I saw Tom. He was standing in front of the French doors that sealed off the seldom used dining room. He looked up at me with that sad, mournful pout that had taken his face the day Ma died and hadn't gone away yet; it made him look less than his eleven years, not like old people in mourning, who always take on age. Only now with his pouting mourning there was a tense look of fright, of bewilderment.

"Uncle Clay is back," he said.

"I know," I said. I could hear them talking behind the doors, Pa and Uncle Clay, their voices just murmurous enough to be indistinct. "Where is Rachel?" I asked.

"Upstairs," Tom said.

I went upstairs and tapped on her door. The way she said, "Come in"—so tense and anxious and even dramatic—made it plain that she knew he was there, thought it was he at the door now. I waited a moment before opening the door. Then I entered. She was sitting on the bed in her white dress, her long slim white arms bare. She was staring at the door, the anticipation bright in her face. Then, without her face moving, the anticipation was gone, the brightness faded out, and she was simply staring; and it was as if a great span of time had elapsed in a single second, shot through world and soul, aging and changing suddenly and swiftly with the same subtlety as it did over the great spans. The dark huddled upon the gray window behind her. Now her face, still unchanged, wore the disappointment of proud women, of women still and proud and hopeful and abeyant since the inception of grief and tragedy; watching me now with that abeyant passion, with that same static unspent passion that I had seen countless times in the face pressed to this upstairs window watching the road, watching day turn into night and then staring endlessly and endlessly into night's wide, somber face.

"You know he's here," I said.

"Yes," she said. "I saw from the window. Then I saw him go with Father into the dining room. I was halfway down the stairs when they closed the doors."

"They haven't seen each other for a long time." I came closer. I could see now the tears in her eyes. She looked back at me, unabashed, unconcealing, as if stating the purest, most sublime happiness, the emotion risen from solitude and loneliness, from faith and forbearance; perhaps more a triumph of faith than a simple happiness, for when he had left the last time Uncle Clay had said, "It's very dangerous where I'm going. Perhaps I won't be back."

She stood up. She was so very tall and beautiful, with long, yellow hair, with heavy red lips that always looked like smiling or crying, depending upon her eyes. At the socials she was the most popular partner, but since Uncle Clay had last gone away she had not danced with anyone, had even stopped going to the socials.

"Do I look presentable, Jeffrey?" she asked.

"You look beautiful," I said.

"Oh, Jeffrey," she said, her eyes closing for a moment. "He's back. Oh, oh, Jeffrey." She came to me and put her hands on my shoulders, looking at me. "You don't know what it is to be in love, do you? You're only sixteen, it hasn't yet happened to you. But someday you'll know. And then you'll know too why your silly sister would cry so. Although you won't cry. Men don't cry, do they? Not over love anyway. Did you see him? How did he look to you?"

"He looks the same," I said.

She closed her eyes again for a moment, intimately seeing him, I knew. Then she looked at me again. "Tell him I'll be here, waiting," she said, removing her hands from me, drawing back, smiling.

I left her and went back downstairs. They were still talking behind the doors, and so I went out to the porch and sat on the top step. I looked again down the road. It was night now. I couldn't see anything down there, but I remembered the way Uncle Clay's face had looked back, and it made that dark seem sinister, as with a lurking, a hidden presence.

Tom had taken Uncle Clay's horse into the stable and was currying him, standing tiptoe to reach the strong, still, graceful back. I could hear him talking to the horse in the dark. Then I heard the doors rolling apart and I turned around. They came through the doors together, Pa with his arm (he had to raise it because he was the shorter) around Uncle Clay's shoulders. Their faces were quite grave which was not uncommon for Pa, but for Uncle Clay was very uncommon; in fact, the only other time I could remember his face being like that was when he came to Ma's burial those two years ago; I had been watching him because I had wanted to do as he did, to cry if he did, to not cry if he didn't.

Now I could hear them talking. It was Pa. "Are you sure you did wise in coming here?" And Uncle Clay: "This was the only place. Perhaps in a day or so. . . ." Then they saw me. Uncle Clay smiled. He walked out from under Pa's arm. I stood up, hooking my thumb into my belt, one foot on the porch, the other on the top step.

"Jeff," Uncle Clay said.

"I saw you ride in," I said.

We went down the porch steps together and walked slowly through the dark.

"Were you south again?" I asked.

"What?" he asked absent-mindedly. He had been peering off into the dark. He looked at me. "What?"

"Were you south again?"

"Yes, part of the time."

"Did you see any of the fighting?"

"Some."

"Where?"

"Oh, Virginia."

"Where? Seven Pines?"

"No, not there. Just some skirmishes. I was busy carrying dispatches."

"For who?"

"The Army."

"You're not in the regular army, are you? I mean you're doing something secret, aren't you?"

He laughed. "If I told you then you would know." He looked at me, his clean beardless face warm and tolerant.

"It is a secret then, isn't it?"

"After the war, then we'll talk about it."

"When do you think it will be over?"

"Oh, soon enough."

"Do you think I'll be able to get into it?"

He didn't answer. He leaned on the fence, folding together his long, supple fingers, gazing off into the dark.

I couldn't sleep that night. I had been so anxious to talk to Uncle Clay, had so many questions to ask that I couldn't wait until the sun came up, and we could ride over the meadows together and talk. I kept getting out of bed and going to the window, much to the disturbance of Tom's sleep. The third time I got out of bed it was after midnight. (I knew it was after midnight because the church bells had already broadcast their farewell tolling out of the belfry and across the farms and fields and graveyards, and it always seemed sacrilegious to be awake after the tolling died away.) I was standing by the window for probably an hour, watching the dark, when I saw something moving in it, something coming along the road, only not walking in the middle of the road but in the ditch at the side, staying close to the trees. I couldn't tell who it was, would probably not have noticed it at all if not for the fact that I had been watching the dark so intently; it was like a shadow, displaced, in motion, in search for a place to alight.

It came all the way up the road, up to the fence, and then it was standing on the fence's lower rail, then swinging one leg over the top, straddling it for a moment like some absurd equestrian figure; and then silently in the yard, moving toward the stable where Uncle Clay's sorrel was and Rachel's mare, Mark, and my horse, Charl, were sleeping too. It was a man, short and, from my upstairs vantage point, rather baggy-looking, as if wearing somebody else's hat and coat and trousers and walking in somebody else's stride, but thinking his own thoughts. Quietly, furtively, he went into the stable.

He did not stay long in the stable. It was probably three breaths. I stood at the window and watched the stable door, and I don't think I drew more than those three breaths before he reappeared, moving out of the stable and into the yard, then over the fence and into the road once more and gone: all done with the unreality of something that comes silently and sourcelessly from the night, with mesmeric stealth and silence, almost as if it had not happened at all; and even the moment he disappeared back into the absorbing sourceless night I had to ask myself if he had really been there; not who he was or what he wanted, but had he really been.

That was the first thing I saw that night. Combined with my restless anxiety to talk to Uncle Clay, it was enough to keep me awake at the window for at least another hour, standing in my nightshirt watching the darkness for a reappearance, watching the sky above the maple for some sign from heaven which I always believed I would see when I stood alone by the window late at night, when everything was quiet and I was alone—some secret symbol of recognition or contiguity which I alone would see and which I would never confess that I had seen, not even to Pete Mariah my best friend.

I was not alarmed though. Probably because Uncle Clay was there. Maybe I had been hoping that the apparition would try to steal something so I could have called Uncle Clay and gone with him in pursuit of it. But the apparition had not done anything, simply gone into the stable and come right out (to look at the horses, of course, to see Uncle Clay's sorrel there and then come back the next day with a mob of men and a rope. But I didn't know that then. I didn't know anything then, only that Uncle Clay was a god and that I wanted to join the Army).

So I stood by the window and watched. No other strangers came out of the dark. But I did see Uncle Clay. That was the second thing. They had gone off for a walk in the pasture when I had gone to bed. But now they were coming out of the barn. At first Rachel's white dress startled me; she looked like some columnar ghost appearing at the barn door. Uncle Clay was behind her. I moved behind the curtains and watched them; I didn't want them to think I was spying. It wasn't spying, either; they had just appeared where I happened to be looking.

They walked slowly across the yard, close to each other. The window was open, the wind coming softly, first through the tree in a long poignant suspiration and then the curtain moved against me in a dreamy languorous billow, and I could hear their voices very small and distant, distant even though they were just under the window. They stopped in the middle of the yard and Rachel's white dress pressed against Uncle Clay and I could see the dark circle that his arms made around her back. Then he released her and they walked again. I kept drawing further back from the window as they neared the house, until my back was flat against the wall and all I could see was the porch steps and Rachel's white dress afloat there. I heard them coming in, heard them on the stairs, heard them pass my door, the floor crackling. Then Rachel's door closed and a moment later, further down the hall, the other door.

3

And they would have done it too—hanged him—if it hadn't been for the Judge. If there was one man in Capstone that the men, armed and angry men too, would listen to it was Judge Stetterson. He was the law and conscience of Capstone. He was in a way an enigmatic person, who professed a certain irreligiousness but who justified the redness of his soul (he said that honest God-fearing folk had warm red souls) by his own scrupulous (but not ruthless) maintenance of the law, his fidelity to law, and maybe this impressed men more than an overt religious devotion; because a man could cheat in his manifestation of religious devotion, but never in his probity and principles when it came to arbitrating and enunciating the law because the law was expressed, decreed for the eyes and ears of men.

So he never sat in church, but he upheld the laws which built and maintained the church; and when some of the church elders who were skeptical of the Judge's not being a skeptic asked him why he spent his Sundays in his book-filled, bachelor-quiet study drinking whiskey, he said, "Just trying out one of the Reverend's theories to see if it really does taste worse on Sunday. And it don't, boys, it really don't."

He came riding up slowly now. He must have been hurrying before, knowing the importance of time. But speed, haste, a frantic face and arm waving, would be the wrong antidote to violence. So he rushed until he came into sight, then came on slowly. He cut his timing rather fine, but he knew his men. His appearance was almost casual, but he was set in that saddle, he was fixed, alert, intent, and furious, holding the reins in one hand, the other hand resting at his side. He watched them as he rode slowly and inevitably up the road.

It was just when they had fitted the noose around Uncle Clay. One of them said, "It's the Judge."

They all looked. He continued to be in no hurry, as if he were riding aimlessly, seeing nothing. It got quiet. I could hear the mild clop-clop-clop of his horse. It was uncanny the way they all stopped and watched him, and how slowly, how casually he came on. He came through the gate and stopped just outside the swoop of the tree. He didn't dismount. He looked quite small on the sturdy white mare, dark-suited, immaculate, unhurried, sitting above them.

A warm breeze stiffened the tree for a moment and then all the leaves rose and fell in a great foamy sighing.

"Does this congregation have a spokesman?" the Judge asked.

It did not, it seemed. The men stood uncomfortably still, eyes down.

"How about you, Adamson?"

"You know why we're doing this, Judge," Adamson said, stubborn, irascible, and still respectful.

"There was no trial."

"We all know what he is."

"We've heard rumors. We don't hang a man for what his neighbors say about him, even though those neighbors might be God-fearing Christians," the Judge said, a sharp edge of sarcasm in his voice.

"Everybody knows about him and them Copperheads in Shantytown, Judge," one of the men said, his voice growling sullenly through a huge black beard.

"Well it might be true then," the Judge said. "But then again it might not. You make a little mistake here now and where are you going to find your forgiveness? And besides that, each man of you that lays hold of that rope will be called to account for it—and there won't be any rumor about *that*." He looked at Uncle Clay for a moment, curiously. Uncle Clay looked back at him; I guess it was the only place he had to look. Now the Judge said, "Sheriff Rice is out of town at the moment. I want two of you men to take Mr. Taylor to the jail."

"Then what?" Adamson asked.

"Then we'll start preparing for a trial," the Judge said.

They demurred. But they were beaten, and they all knew it. One of them removed the noose from Uncle Clay and then cut loose his wrists. Then two of them put him into a wagon and with the Judge began riding back down the road. The others, sullen and disgruntled, began mounting their horses and riding off in their different directions, down the road or through the trees or across the pasture, angry men, beaten by something they could neither understand nor resist.

Pa was standing up then, one hand on his chest, the pitchfork lying on the ground.

"There," I said, looking at Rachel. "They couldn't hang him."

"Yes they could," she said, staring at the empty yard, her eyes hard, flat, disillusioned.

The rope hung emptily from the tree, the zero of noose swaying in the dusky wind.

CHAPTER 2

The next morning I heard the sounds, loud and angry, a relentless primitive rhythm. The sun had just come into the room, flooding through the pale curtains. I got out of bed and looked out the window. Pa was in the yard, at the tree, his legs braced, swinging the ax savagely and desperately against the tree; with all his strength swinging the ax back and forth across his chest, his body shuddering and going rigid at each ringing impact. Each time he cut he had to jerk the ax free, pulling it with thrusts out of the mighty, indomitable trunk.

When I had dressed and gone downstairs he had stopped. He was standing next to the tree, panting, the ax handle in his hand, the head lying on the ground. He had achieved some little damage upon the tree, having chipped some bark splinters, the yellow wood showing cleanly underneath.

"It would take a man six months to put this damned tree down," he said, looking up into it, his eyes white, somber as they studied the soaring mass of leaves and twigs and boughs that were like some cloud of dark conflagration. "But maybe it's better if we leave her stand." He looked at me. I picked up the axhead and handed it to him. He tried to fit it back onto the helve, but it had broken clean off. He looked at the tree. "She's got a hide of iron," he muttered.

"I'll help you take it down," I said.

"No. No. We'll let her be, even though she would have hung your Uncle Clay. It's a mean, evil tree. But we'll let her be. We'll let God take care of her."

Rachel came out of the barn. She was wearing boots and breeches and a man's shirt. Her hair was not combed.

"Why did you stop?" she demanded.

He showed her the pieces of the ax. She looked at the tree.

"It's a horrible thing," she said. "It frightens me, gives me the horrors. I've always hated it. Since I was a child. It's horrible and it's ugly. All those branches . . . like witches' fingers . . . grasping . . . always trying to reach you. And at night, how it is always whispering . . . even when there is no wind . . . saying things that no one understands. It should be destroyed . . . cut down . . . burned. . . ."

"It should," Pa said.

The old maple was an ugly legend in Capstone. It was said that at least six men had been hanged on it, going all the way back to the days of the Revolution; that because it had always been the biggest and the strongest tree it had always been chosen as the gallows. The victims had been thieves and murderers and once a man who had committed adultery. And now many people were ashamed of it and made a point of not speaking of it, and perhaps it would have been chopped down long ago except that someone had come and built a house here and cleared the land; but it seemed that not even that could change or eradicate the malevolent heritage that ran like warped strength through the thick grotesque limbs that had come within seconds of cracking Uncle Clay's neck.

"But if it stands," Pa said, "we'll always remember what they tried to do."

"I would prefer to forget," Rachel said.

She went into the house. Pa watched her.

"She'd have rather seen him hung like a man than kick for his life like he did," he said, half-amused, half-embittered, his somber eyes small and blue and keen in his bearded face.

"What will they do to him now?" I asked.

Pa sighed. "I don't know. They've gone about telling so many evil lies about him."

"What sort of lies?"

"What difference does it make?" Pa said angrily. "A lie is a lie. Once you've broken a Christian precept, no matter how trifling that infraction, then it's a sin. And it's a day and age now when people listen to lies, to slanders. It's the beginning of the end of the Christian era," Pa said heatedly, resentfully, his eyes fixed upon me. "In our own land brother is slaughtering brother. Here," he said, showing me the broken ax. "Here is your symbol." He let the severed halves fall to the ground.

But I wasn't concerned about any of that, not the decline of the Christian era nor the vision of the slaughter of brother by brother. I was concerned about Uncle Clay. Later that morning I rode up the hill into town, hitched Charl to the post outside the Dooley House where all the men were sitting on the porch staring at me. I stared back at them. Some of them had been among the mob yesterday. I waited for one of them to say something, but they only stared.

I went down the street toward the sheriff's office where the jail was. It was a peculiar building, with a wooden roof and brick walls, a rather squat, oblong building which was used mainly as a place to put the drunks when they were making too much noise or had fallen asleep in the street. It was not far from Bumper Clark's blacksmith shop where the Judge occasionally convened court. I could hear Bumper's anvil clanging as I went up the steps and into the sheriff's office.

Sheriff Rice was there, sitting at the desk.

"Hello, Jeff," he said, smiling amiably behind his mustache. He was a large, good-humored man, the strongest, most fearless man in Capstone—which was why they had made him sheriff—and, next to Uncle Clay, the quickest and deadliest with a gun.

"I want to see my uncle," I said.

"Can't let you do that. I'm not letting anyone near him, not even his kin."

There was a closed door. Behind it was a dim, narrow passageway with six cells. I had seen them once. They were very small and malodorous, each with a low narrow cot as their lone article of furniture.

"Is he all right?" I asked.

"Clay Taylor is always all right, it seems," the sheriff said almost wistfully, regretfully, as if Uncle Clay's always being all right was something of a nuisance to him.

"Why is he in jail?"

"Don't you know, Jeff?"

"I don't know."

The sheriff sighed. He was reluctant. He gazed down at his clasped fingers, then back up at me.

"I don't suppose your Pa would tell you," he said. "Though I don't suppose your Pa believes it anyway. Your Pa thinks there's no one like his brother Clay. First God, then Clay. I suppose you think the same, you and Rachel and Tom. I can see why too. Clay is the type of man that other men either desperately hate or fiercely envy, and probably both at the same time too. Ever since Clay was a boy—"

"What's he done?" I asked. I didn't want to listen to the sheriff's monologue about Uncle Clay. I knew all about Uncle Clay, even more than the sheriff knew. Uncle Clay had taught me to ride and to shoot, and when a man has done those things for you, with you, there is very little that you don't know about him.

"He's been in the employ of the Confederate Government."

"It's a lie."

Patiently, kindly, the sheriff said, "No, Jeff. It's the truth. He was caught once, carrying dispatches for the Northern Virginia Army. He got away but he'd been seen. He was seen, as a prisoner, by a man from Capstone. He didn't know until he got back to Capstone that he had been identified—otherwise you can rest assured he'd never have come back. I know you don't want to believe it, and that it's kind of hard to take, but when you stop to remember that your uncle lived in South Carolina for two years before the war. . . ."

But I wouldn't let it happen. I fought to keep the roof of my world intact, to resist the threatening collapse and the influx of unbearable darkness.

"You see, they're all mistaken," I said, my voice low now, talking in a hurry. "They don't know the truth of it. Maybe I shouldn't be telling this, but Uncle Clay was doing secret work for the Government; so secret that he wouldn't even tell me or Pa about it. He can't tell any of it till the war's over."

The sheriff didn't say anything. He just looked at me and I felt like a child.

I went out then. The sun was shining brightly, summer hot on the Grant Avenue dust. A few wagonfuls of produce rolled by, the farmers shaking the reins over their horses' backs. I watched them go down the incline, past the pine trees, dipping and vanishing as if into a sea. I started to go back to Charl but then changed my mind, remembering something—the little barred windows that faced the trees behind the jail. I walked around behind the jail and stood in the yard gazing up at the little windows that looked like dark, blank faces contemplating in severe gloom the dust of blasted panoramas. They were ugly openings in the brick wall, too high for the occupants of the cells to peer through without standing on something. The sunlight was bright and hard against the wall.

I took the rain barrel from the end of the building and moved it to beneath one of the windows. Mounting it and putting my fingers around the rough, rusted bars I peered into the first cell. It was empty. I got off and moved the barrel further down. I had to peer into four cells before I found Uncle Clay. He was lying on the cot, on his side, staring at the wall. I just stared at him for a moment. He looked so different, so sad, the walls and the bars around him, the sun etching the bars on the floor where his boots were standing. There was a strong odor, like fruit that has rotted. He looked so forlorn there, cast out, as if even his thoughts could not escape his cell.

When I said his name he looked up. For a moment he was startled by my face and my curled fingers on the bars. Then he smiled, slowly, a dark, sly smile. When he stood up his head was about a foot below the window. He reached up and touched my hand, the arrested smile fixed on his lips. He said quietly,

"I knew I could count on you, Jeff."

Then I knew that I was going to help him, that that was what I had come there for. I hadn't known it before. But Uncle Clay knew it, had been waiting for me, waiting to trust me.

"What are they going to do?" I asked.

"I don't know," he said. "And I don't intend to wait around and see." He brought his hand down and stared up at me, his eyes sharp, even, as if taking my measure. "I can depend on you, Jeff, can't I?" he asked.

I nodded, holding tightly to the bars.

"I have to get out of here tonight," he said. He looked back over his shoulder for a moment. Then he moved closer beneath the window, his voice lowered almost to inaudibility. "My pistols are in my room. Get them. Then come back here tonight with my horse. Give me the pistols and leave the horse at the side of the jail. Have you got that?"

"Yes," I said. He made me repeat what he had instructed me to do, then he asked,

"Can you do it?"

"Yes," I said.

"Wait until it's good and dark before you come back."

"How will you get out?"

"Leave that to me. And don't say a word to anyone. Not even your Pa."

I didn't tell Pa. But I had to tell somebody. Not that I couldn't handle it alone, not that; but that it seemed to be of such terrific magnitude that I felt overwhelmed by the whole idea of it—overwhelmed and impressed and too afraid to think about being afraid, because it was me helping Uncle Clay, doing something for him, getting him out of a bad situation, saving his life. I was suddenly in a strange and not unembarrassing position. I felt deeply empowered and humble and determined.

When I came home I left Charl in the stable and wandered out into the pasture to be alone to think about my problem; and indeed it was a problem, as simple as the technical aspects of it might have appeared. But lest the simplicity of it deceive me, I sat quietly and pondered, to be certain of every move I was to make; to conjure, if possible, the unforeseen.

A breeze came, soft and low across the pasture. I could see it coming, bending the grasstops in tiny shivering waves and then sweeping overhead in a grander gesture into the trees, and a leaf was detached, the first that I had seen fall that summer and I stared at it where it lay and interpreted it as an omen, an omen of good, just as I always interpreted a shooting star as a benediction of some kind or clouds in a pool as augurs of good fortune. The fallen leaf was still green except for a few rust spots. No other fell, although the breeze stirred them all; and it was as if the leaf had been sacrificial, its fall decreed by the breeze's Scriptural command.

But these divine allusions still did not help to fully allay my apprehensions which were not fear but merely the natural misgivings of approaching great adventure. So I told Pete Mariah. Pete was the best friend I had in Capstone, and although most of the older people disapproved of him and the ones his own age didn't quite trust him as people that age have to trust their friends, I had always found him a willing and dependable, even if unpredictable, friend.

Pete lived with his parents and five sisters in an old frame house near the marsh. His father worked as bookkeeper for the Meyer dairy farm and was a man who despaired too much and too often for too many things, beginning with the state of his own health and all the way down to the state of health of Meyer's cows. Pete's mother was a small, pale woman who banked everything on religion (including Pete's salvation, although this sometimes seemed hardly worth the effort), she slept with a Bible under her pillow; but she could never get Pete to go to church, not with plea nor threat nor bribe, not that Pete was antichurch, but just that he was the type that on Sunday mornings during Mass liked to climb up and look in the windows at the other youths, who were compelled to sit on the sticky wooden benches, and make faces at those youths.

We were the same age, Pete and I. He liked to hunt and

fish and used to stay away from home for two or three days at a time, not that he was ever that far away, but that he just liked to lay down on the ground under the stars, he said. We were about the same in everything except that he couldn't ride a horse as well and had very little experience at working. He was a moody fellow who thrived on sudden bursts of enthusiasm. Under a shock of wild brown hair that hung down on all sides of his head, he had a thin, disinterested face that some people took as being that of a moron and others as indicative of deep intellectual resources; but all those people were wrong; what Pete was didn't show in his face: he was shrewd. And on top of all that wild, brown hair he always wore—lately—a Union forage cap that Uncle Clay had brought back for him. Once when Pete cut his hand, he let some of the blood run on the hat and after that went around telling people that the hat had belonged to a soldier who had been shot through the head.

I knew that if I wanted to find Pete the last place to go was to his house. So late that afternoon I walked up to town to look for him. His town haunts were the blacksmith shop and the place under Dooley's porch where he would sit and listen to the men talk (sometimes he heard the damndest things there and because of them had got to know all of the town's loose women; in fact, it got to such a point that the men, before saying anything spicy or otherwise private, would go down off the porch and bend down to see if Pete was sitting there), and the back yard of Gibson's tavern where he would sit and talk to the old Negro cook, and I went to them all and couldn't find him. I went to the other side of town then. He had a favorite spot there in an elm grove where the stream ran, and that was where I found him. He was sitting under one of the trees, his overalled legs drawn up before him, gazing over his knees at the stream, smoking a pipe, the forage cap pulled forward over his eyes, bits of brown hair sticking out from under the visor. When he saw me he squinted one eye and said,

"Hello, Deacon." He would call people that, everyone except the man in town whose name really was Deacon, Benjamin Deacon. He called him Rabbi.

I sat down next to him.

"It was my ambition to fish today," Pete said, "but my state of mind forbids it."

"What's wrong with your state of mind?" I asked.

"It tends to make me stationary."

"Well you've got to change that," I said. "Uncle Clay needs help."

He looked at me, squinting one eye, a characteristic which would make him look both very interested and very mistrustful at the same time. The mention of Uncle Clay had aroused him though.

"Clay needs help?"

"He's in the jail. I suppose you've heard what they tried to do yesterday?"

"I heard. That's people for you, in a nutshell. They find somebody who's a better man than any of them are so they've got to hang him."

"I talked to him this morning. He thinks he can get out, if we help him."

"We'll help him," Pete said, excited now. "What do we have to do?"

"Well it's pretty simple," I said. "He wants his pistols handed to him through the bars, and his horse standing around at the side."

"When?"

"Tonight."

Pete looked up at the sky, pushing back the cap. "Well it's going to be dark soon enough, Deacon. Maybe we ought to start now."

"We've got time."

"People can never afford to say that," Pete said, standing up. He rapped his pipe against the tree until all the tobacco had spilled out. Then he put the pipe into his shirt pocket.

We began to walk away from the stream, through the elm grove. The late afternoon shadows were beginning to grow.

"I heard what they've been saying," Pete said.

"It's not true," I said.

"They've all got it in for him because he's been a fast man with their women."

It made me think for a moment about what I had seen from my window two nights ago, but I didn't want to think about that because maybe it wasn't true. Pete suddenly guffawed and clapped his hands sharply together.

"What's the matter?" I asked.

"Clay Taylor's going to bust jail!" he said exultantly.

And as it turned out it was a good thing that we took that early start, because we were going to need all the time we could get. We went back to the farm to get everything set. It was just dusk then, the sun leaving a hard copper light on the meadows. We passed a few men on their way home from the rope factory. Coming down the hill we could see the last of daylight between the branches of the tree. When seen from the hill the tree looked three times the size of the house, bigger than the house and the barn and the stable all three together—a gnarled dark mass, and it made me think how futile it had been for Pa to try and cut it down.

They had just finished supper. Rachel had gone up to her room, to sit by the window and think about Uncle Clay, I knew. Tom was in the barn with the cows. Pa was sitting in the living room where he always sat, under Ma's picture; just sitting there, thinking about Uncle Clay too. If I would have said anything he would have started again with the stories, about all the wondrous things that Uncle Clay had done: the fights, the horse races, the feats of marksmanship and strength and daring, and "just the way he would come into a room"—how you knew that here was someone special. They were so completely different in everything: appearance, personality, outlook. Perhaps Uncle Clay had brought to life Pa's own dream of himself. Uncle Clay was the knight and the duelist and the philanderer and the engaging scoundrel who looked upon friends and enemies alike with the same aloof, condescending charm—things which Pa would have condemned in any other man probably. Pa had raised Uncle Clay after their parents had been killed in a fire in Manhattan where they had lived then. Not many people in Capstone knew it, but Clay was not really Pa's brother. Pa's mother had died and his father had taken Clay's mother as his second wife, giving her infant son, Clay, his name. The fire occurred several years later, so Clay had never known his real father and known his mother only so slightly that he had ceased to remember her. So although Pa became like a father to him he could not call Clay son, and thus they became brothers. He had brought Uncle Clay (I had never referred to him as anything but Uncle) to Capstone with him and bought the farm and worked it day and night; and at the same time brought up Uncle Clay who was fifteen years younger, and not just brought him up but saw him grow into the tall, strong, exciting, proficient person he was today. So in later years I guess Pa did regard Uncle Clay, as some people said, as half brother and half son.

But I didn't say anything. I didn't want to hear the stories now. Pete remained outside on the porch while I went upstairs to Uncle Clay's room to get the pistols. But the pistols weren't there. I looked in all the drawers and in the closet and in the trunk. I searched everything, everywhere. Then I went to Rachel's room. When I knocked she said, "Go away," but I opened the door and went in. She was sitting at the window, turned in her chair looking at me.

"Where are his pistols?" I asked.

"Pa has them. Why? Are you going to get him out?" She asked this not with hope or anticipation but more with curiosity.

"Maybe. Where are the pistols?"

"Pa took them. I saw him coming out of the room with them this morning. I don't know what he's done with them."

"All right," I said. I began to close the door, but before I did, something prompted me to say, "Don't you want to see him get out?"

There was a strange, hurt look in her face, as though something had come from afar to sting her. "Yes," she said quietly. "Do whatever you can for him."

I went downstairs. Coming down I could see Pa sitting under the picture, grave and withdrawn, unapproachable. I kept going, through the room and out to the porch, conscious of his eyes following me, those grave withdrawn eyes that always seemed to have seen all of sorrow's fervent reapings, to have seen the martyrizing of the saints and pondered the gloom of failing heartbeats.

I didn't tell Pete until we got into the stable.

"Can't you ask your Pa for them?" Pete asked.

"I'd have to tell him what I wanted them for and Uncle Clay said not to tell him."

"But it's an emergency."

"I know," I said fretfully. I looked outside. The last of daylight was gone from between the branches of the maple. Time seemed not to be passing now but to have stopped, hung in massive suspension, to move again suddenly with a roll and a crash, not when the sun came but when I had either succeeded or failed.

"He can't get out of there without a pistol," Pete said.

"I know."

"We're going to have to get one from someplace else."

"From where?" I asked.

"Do you know Clint Peady, the old man who is night watchman down at the lumber yard?"

"I know him."

"Well he's got a pistol, although he's too old to be much good with it anymore."

"Will he give it to us?" I asked.

Pete had already begun walking off into the darkness. He was through the stable door.

"Of course he won't," he said irascibly.

We went down to the lumber yard which was two miles off, just the other side of the creek. We had to cross a small footbridge which could be very dangerous if you weren't careful because it was narrow and wobbly and had no rail on either side, though the creek wasn't quite so deep at the moment, there having been a drought most of the summer.

Clint Peady sat in the shack there all night, a doddering symbol of authority. He was a thin little old man with a long white mustache and short white beard who generally fell asleep on the job an hour or so after he sat down and snored away most of the night. Pete claimed that the old man had a pistol, supplied by the people who hired him, that he had seen it once when the old man chased him from trying to appropriate some planks.

We had no difficulty in getting over the fence into the yard. The watchman's shack stood at the far end of it. We stole quietly across the dirt toward the shack, moving with the stealth of Indians in the still, moonless night, coming up to the window. Looking in we could see Clint Peady asleep in a wooden chair, his head fallen forward over his chest as if he were in prayer, asleep so peacefully that you could have got the impression that armed guards were about. He wore a hard hat and a suit of blue broadcloth and red flannel tie. I noted all of that, but I didn't see a pistol around anywhere.

"Are you sure he's got one?" I asked, whispered as we huddled before the lighted window.

Pete didn't say anything. He was deep in concentration. I followed him around to the door. Noiselessly he got it open. The first thing he did was tiptoe over to the table and blow out the lamp, leaving the shack in total darkness. Peady was snoring in placid rhythms as if his franchise to sleep had been issued by Morpheus himself, hands in lap, head still dropped forward. I watched the old man while Pete moved around the shack looking for the pistol, moving quietly through the dark, the army cap fixed on his head, his face grimly determined, as if there was a bayonet charge in the offing.

Looking at the old man I wondered what would happen, what we would do, if he woke up—run or collapse and hide or intimidate him. The thought inspired a nervous fear and having no solution at hand, I left it to subconscious speculation. Pete would think of something to do, I knew, and that thought caused me more discomfort than the previous. And then the old man did begin to stir. I watched him, fascinated and afraid as his head began to nod in some deep soporific acquiescence that was becoming crankier each second. Pete came up behind him with a piece of rope. Still I watched, unwilling to move, intrigued by what was happening in the dark, as if it had nothing to do with me. Pete looped the rope around the old man's chest and pulled it around behind the chair and deftly bound the old man into it. Then with other pieces of rope he tied the old man's legs to the legs of the chair. It wasn't until he had lifted off Peady's hat and thrust a bandanna around his eyes that the old man awoke, and awoke with a start and a yelp, pulling forward startled and amazed in the ropes, squirming and rattling in the chair, good and caught.

"Help!" he cried. "Who are yeh?"

"Shut your mouth," Pete growled in a heavily disguised voice that made me whirl to see who had spoken.

The old man, his arms and legs bound, his eyes blindfolded, desisted and fell obediently and alertly silent at the sound of the strange voice. Pete stood behind him. Pete swallowed, clearing his throat, and I knew he was going to bring the voice back.

"Where's your pistol, old man?"

"It ain't here," Peady's stiff, scared voice said.

"Where is it?"

"It's home."

"Home?"

"I swear."

"You telling us the truth, old man?"

"I swear it."

Pete drew away and came to me, putting his hand on my shoulder and whispering into my ear.

"He lives just the other side of the creek," he said.

I looked at him. Then I looked at old Clint Peady who was sitting stiff and straight, bound not just by the ropes but by mortal fear as well, as if he was expecting sudden, unwarned annihilation.

"We've got to have that pistol," I whispered.

That was all Pete wanted to hear. He went back to his prisoner, Peady's head jerking sideways at the sound of the crackling floor board. Pete swallowed again, his head sinking for a moment into his shoulders to gather the voice, and then the voice came again.

"You sure the pistol ain't here?"

"I swear," Peady said. "It's in my house."

"Then we'll go there," the voice said. "Now you keep your mouth shut or we'll cut your throat." And he made the threat sound genuine. Pete came back to me. "We can't take a chance on leaving him here," he whispered. "We'd better take him along."

"How?" I asked.

"We'll carry him in the chair. It ain't so far."

"Suppose somebody sees us?"

"There ain't nobody around here this time of night."

So, after another desperate warning was growled, we lifted up the chair along with its tense, frightened prisoner. Pete took the legs and I took hold from the back and we carried Peady out of the shack and across the yard, past the piles and piles of planks that gave the impression of a curious throng paused to watch the strange procession pass. We opened the gate and marched out like that, like two Hindu bearers toting their wheezy maharajah. We bumped along clumsily through the dark, old Peady rattling breathlessly in the chair, not really knowing what we wanted or where we were going or what we were going to do, conjuring the darkest fears, I'm sure. Once the bandanna began to slip down and we had to put him down and tighten it, tightening it real good this time.

When we got onto the footbridge and began going over the creek Peady became terribly frightened. Below he could hear the creek swirling and his fright became intolerable. He began to squirm and then struggle. Pete told him to stop, but he didn't, or couldn't. The chair began to sway like a hammock. We should have put him down and tried to calm him and maybe we would have, but it was happening too quickly. He got one leg loose and kicked at Pete, hitting him in the stomach. Startled, Pete dropped his end of the chair and the impact made me loosen my grip and I let go too and for a moment old Peady was sitting there and the chair was tilted over on two legs and for that moment we both just looked at him wondering if it would go or not, amazed and fascinated and paralyzed; and then the chair began to lean way over and Peady's struggling wasn't helping it any. Then the chair was in mid-air, the old man sitting there blindfolded with his hands tied behind him and the one leg kicking out, sitting horizontally now just over the water too astonished to cry out yet, not crying out until he struck the water; and then his mewling cry was lost because the splash was loud, it sounded enormous, and two marvelous plumes of water rose up, one soaring off and back into the creek, the other flattening upon the bridge with a splat.

For a moment we saw the legs of the chair and the legs of the old man sticking up out of the water, and that was all; but then the chair righted itself with an upswoop and the old man reappeared, still blindfolded, still sitting in his ropes, and yelling now. The chair swirled around in a brief whirlpool and then bobbed and bowed and the legs appeared again—the chair's and the man's—sticking up straight, floating mysteriously; and then the old man swooped up again and this time his yelling was not quite so loud. The chair spun around again and for a moment he was sitting quite properly, quite decorously upon the water and as he floated under the bridge another yell was washed out and when we ran to the other side he was just reappearing again, shaking the water from him, floating now with the sure, strong tide.

"He'll sail right out to the damned East River!" Pete

cried. Then Pete and I were stretched out in the dark, over the water like streaks, then hitting it, not making as much noise as when the old man and the chair had gone in, swimming furiously toward him, watching the legs reaching up again and then the old man coming back, spinning around, facing us, then facing toward the river, rocking, bobbing, sailing forward into the dark and I had the terrifying feeling that we would never be able to reach him, even though we were almost on him now, my hand reaching out just in time to spare him another dunking. Pete swam around in front of him to keep him upright while I began pushing the chair toward the bank, the dark, cold water brawling all around us. The old man was too frightened to be able to muster any noises except a blowing sound he kept making with his mouth that was probably his breathing. He just sat there bolt upright and I believe he would have sat and looked the same even if it weren't for the ropes. But we weren't forgetting the ropes or the bandanna either; Pete had the presence of mind to make sure the bandanna did not come down. A tree branch came floating by, slow and placid, and it seemed to be regarding us with haughty curiosity. Then I felt bottom and in another moment I was on my feet and we were pulling the chair up the bank, the old man sitting like stone in it, but then he began to cough and to spit water, shaking his head, the water running through his beard.

We pulled him up the bank and then let him sit for a moment while we looked at each other. Pete's finger was up against his lips, warning me not to speak. Then he frowned and I knew the voice was coming again.

"You all right, old man?"

"Hell, no!" the old man croaked.

Then we picked him up and carried him again.

Peady's house wasn't far from the creek. It was a one-story clapboard where he lived with his wife, who was probably asleep inside now because we couldn't see any lights. We carried the old man under some trees just beyond his picket fence and put the chair down. He sneezed a few times. I took my handkerchief and wiped some of the water from his face.

"I'm glad to see there's a Christian among yeh," he said sourly.

Pete (his army cap was still fixed upon his head—not even the creek had been able to get it off—the visor glistening with water) was studying the house, completely indifferent to his saturated condition; his fingers pinching under his chin, his underlip pushed out. Then he looked at the old man and I knew the voice was coming again.

"Who's inside the house?"

"What house?" the blindfolded old man asked, jerking up his head as if to try and see from underneath the bandanna.

"We're outside of your house."

"Just my wife's inside," Peady said.

"Sleeping?"

"How should I know, with this damn rag over my eyes?" the old man said petulantly.

"Where's the pistol?"

"It's in my drawer."

"Which room?"

"The bedroom," Peady said.

"Which is the bedroom?" Pete asked.

"The one with the curtains," Peady said.

Pete drew me aside, away from the old man.

"I'll go in after the pistol," he whispered. "You stay here and make sure he keeps still."

"No," I said. "Clay is my uncle. I ought to do it."

"You're too clumsy. You'd wake her up."

"All the same—" I said, tried to say, but it was no good. He was already going toward the house. I went back to the old man and let him know I was standing there. I watched Pete get the window open, lifting it silently, as far as his arms would go, then hoist himself up, sitting on the sill, getting first one leg over and then the other, disappearing through the white curtains into the room.

I waited. And Clint Peady waited, throwing an occasional sneeze. I began to shiver. A cool breeze had begun to blow in from the river, crossing the river from Manhattan, making me shiver in my wet clothes. My shoes felt enormous and filled with water, stiff and heavy, creaking every time I moved. Water was still dripping out of my hair. Above, the trees were murmuring in the breeze that had just passed through Manhattan's close little streets and buildings, over the smoky lamps and the carriages and the cobblestones, past all those ceaseless people and through the smoke and the odors, purifying itself over the river; sailing now over Capstone, the meadows and the trees and the scattered farmhouses where men were smoking their evening pipes and drinking their last glasses and getting ready for bed; soon it would pass the jail and Uncle Clay would hear it in the trees: cool and swift and as sure and as inexorable as if it were being sucked back into some tiny bottle that lay on the Montauk sands.

I watched the window. The curtains were fluttering in

and out, long and loose. It seemed like a long time, but it was probably no longer than three or four minutes before Pete reappeared in the window. First one leg, then the other, and he was sitting on the sill, his legs hanging down. He had the pistol. He was grinning, waving it. I swung my arm at him, but he continued to sit there, grinning and waving. The old man said,

"For damn's sake, untie me."

"Shhh," I hissed at him, trying to sound like a cutthroat. Then I turned back to Pete. That was when the gun went off. He was pointing it straight up. He had been about to let himself drop to the ground and had tensed for the fall and his finger (why he had it laying against the trigger was something beyond explanation, almost beyond sanity) had released the trigger. The pistol went *Bam!* with a white flash like lightning. The old man, probably thinking this was to be his portion for speaking out, screamed that he was dead although that bullet was going straight up to the stars harmless except for all the noise it made and the chair went over backward and I was looking at his shoes. The pistol's kick threw Pete backward too and when I whirled around again I saw his shoes too, halfway up the open window as if he was being slid out feet first, only he was going back in and with a crash. The next scream came from Mrs. Peady, loud and fierce like from an insane asylum and it never stopped. Then the curtains came swooshing out veiling Pete's diving figure, headfirst now as though flung by the screaming. The curtains sailed back off of him as he thudded to the ground and rolled over and leaped up all in the one motion like an acrobat, running at me with his hat in one hand and the pistol in the other, his face white as a ghost's, glaring at me as if I were on fire. He never broke stride nor direction, leaping over the chaired Clint Peady whose legs were still sticking out and whose voice kept insisting he was dead although he was nothing more than very scared and very wet.

With a backward glance toward the flying curtains where Mrs. Peady, a massive figure in white, was dominating with a lusty screaming that must have opened the waters of the creek, I too fled, trying to catch Pete's incredible streaking figure.

It was a mile of running on a dirt road before I caught up to him, or until he finally stopped. He was panting. We both stopped, both panting, for a moment unable to speak. He was holding the pistol slack in his hand. His hat was turned askew, the visor tipped down over one eye. I took the gun from his hand.

"I got it, didn't I?" he gasped defensively.

"All right," I said, gasping too, tucking the pistol into my belt.

He was taking mighty gulping breaths, each threatening to collapse his body as he expelled them. We stood silently for a moment until our breathing partially recomposed itself. Then we began walking along the road, wet, weary.

"It was an accident," Pete said. He was quite subdued, quite contrite, something he seldom was.

I said nothing.

"You won't tell Clay," he said.

"No," I said. "But I can't help thinking there could have been an easier, quieter, drier way."

We walked back up to the farm. The lamps were out by this time, both upstairs and down. I told Pete to come around through the back, in case Rachel was sitting at the window. We came around behind the barn and slipped into the dark, close, animal-smelling stable. Uncle Clay's sorrel was asleep in its stall. We could hear it breathing on the straw, hard and peaceful. I entered the stall and kneeled and put my hand on its hard, relaxed flank. I said, whispered, "Get up. Get up." Slowly his head turned up, looking around at me. He made a sound with his nostrils and I rose and drew back against the wall as slowly, mysteriously, and majestically, he rose in the dark, emerging tall and still from the hissing straw—hind legs, forelegs, his hard firm flanks quivering, throwing his long fine head from side to side for a moment, pawing restively at the straw. I led him from the stall.

In a few minutes we were ready. I mounted via the stirrup, Pete got on behind me by climbing up onto the stall railing. Then we trotted out, ducking as we passed through the door. We rode through the yard and out the gate and down the wagonwheel-rutted road, moving in a canter, our legs jouncing against the taut reddish flanks, and it felt very good sitting astride the sure, strong horse, the wind coming into my face; the trees, the occasional houses slipping by in the deep still night which seemed built around us like a tunnel, walled impenetrably on both sides but open and irresistible ahead; some of the full-leafed branches slapping at us as we went by, the dark road flowing patient and constant beneath the soft cluttering hoofs; and then the road beginning to steepen, the slope beginning, and the horse taking an extra leg of speed, his head held up, carried proud, mane aflutter. We crested the hill, riding easier then. Pete sat silently behind, holding to the cantle.

I could feel the pistol stuck into my belt, pressing against me like a stiff hand of obligation. I had not even looked at it, didn't know what it looked like. But soon it would be in Uncle Clay's hands and with it he would free himself; and I would have been part of it, the escape, the adventure. I felt now as though all my life I had been being groomed for this opportunity, that every breath and moment had been moving with direct and inevitable purpose toward this night, that all knowledge and experience had distilled and crystallized to a degree where I was now capable and trustworthy. Because now Uncle Clay was waiting in the dark for the horse and the pistol, not for me, not waiting in despairing uncertainty thinking over and over: *Will he come?* but knowing that I would be there; so confident that he was thinking no doubt only of what he must do when I pass the weapon into his hands; thinking of escape and freedom and the dark places of his flight. And not just any man there waiting for me, trusting me, but Uncle Clay.

So everything was different this night, this ride. In my heart I could feel it, the change, the strangeness; the heart changing with the body, the mind. Nothing was going to be the same ever again, not myself nor the things around me nor the world at large; I would come as a man now to a world I had never seen. I thought of the men who sat on Dooley's porch, the men who worked the farms and drank ale and whiskey in the tavern—the way they walked and the way they sat their horses; always different from the way I was, and now I began to feel like them, could feel the change in my face, the way my eyes were staring and my lips set together, and it was as if the earth were changing too, swelling, rising to meet the new growth, pathing infinitely toward the stars.

We passed no one, saw no one. When the Grant Avenue buildings came in sight, shaping in flat- and saddle-roofs and steeples out of the night, with lights and the beginning of the sound of people, we slowed.

"We'd better get down," I said, beginning to rein in.

We dismounted. We went through some pines and crossed the avenue about a quarter mile up from the Dooley House. Some men passed near in a buckboard but they didn't see us, or if they did were not interested. We circled very wide behind the jail, coming toward it from the back through the trees. Then we could see the jail, the back wall with the six tiny windows and I thought of Uncle Clay waiting and how good he was going to feel when he saw my face through the bars; and we went on through the trees and the bushes and the ringing crickets.

Pete went around and out to the avenue. I waited in the trees with the horse, my hand resting on the handle of the pistol. I could see the lights in the Dooley House, on the porch and in the windows. Beyond that was the tavern. Several men were sitting on the bench there. Then Pete came back, moving through the dark like a shadow.

"The deputy's in there," he said.

"Casey?"

"There's only one deputy."

"I'm glad it's not the sheriff," I said.

I led the horse around to the side of the building. Pete stayed with him while I went back to the jail, to the window.

I moved the rain barrel over again (I had moved it away before in order to prevent any possible suspicions) and climbed up on it. I looked into the dark cell. I couldn't see anything. It was so black, so cavern-like, I felt for a moment as though I would never be able to find him, to let him know I was there. But when I whispered his name the dark seemed to come alive with him, his presence, his restless seething nearness, even though I couldn't see him.

"Jeff," his voice said, low, intense. (It was more as though the dark—the whole vast infinite invisible dark—had said it.) His fingers appeared on the bars, folding around them, white, hard. Then his face was before me, completing the desperate portrait.

"I couldn't get your pistols," I said. "But I got this one." I handed it to him through the bars, one of the white hands opening to receive it. "The horse is around at the side, where you said. Pete Mariah is there with it."

"All right," Uncle Clay said, almost absently, looking at the pistol. "Now go home." He never said thanks, he never acknowledged, and I understood, because that was the way of men; his gratitude was none the less for its muteness.

But we didn't go home, of course. We went into the trees and hid there, trembling with excitement. From the trees we could hear Uncle Clay calling Casey, his voice innocuous, conversational. Then we heard Casey's voice risen suddenly in surprise and protest, and just as suddenly fallen as Uncle Clay ordered him to be still. There was the snap and clash of an iron door and I stared at the jail's length, the blood hot and throbbing in my temples; trying to picture what he was doing now; the jail seemed tensed for a detonation. And then he appeared around the corner, tall and running, just pushing the pistol down into his belt, never breaking stride, the dark flowing off of him like water. He leaped into the saddle, spun the horse and with a mighty leap broke into full gallop, going down the back road that ran parallel with Grant Avenue almost to the creek.

We were running then, out of the trees and into the road and then down the road after the fast-fading roar of hoof-beats, running after him buoyant and excited, our chests swollen out, our doubled fists pumping, running until he was gone (he was gone in a matter of seconds actually, but he really wasn't gone for us until we couldn't run any longer), until we couldn't pull air any more, stopping in the middle of the dark, silent empty road that seemed as solemnly still as though Roman Legions had just marched by. I put my arm around Pete's shoulders, the both of us staring breathlessly into the wild endless night where Uncle Clay and his horse had stormed into silence.

CHAPTER 3

I was just coming in from the pasture when I saw the Judge riding up the road. He was coming very slowly, deliberate, the way he had ridden the other day to stop the mob. I took one look and ran back down the porch steps and across the yard into the barn. I climbed up the ladder into the loft and lay down in the hay and watched through the window.

The Judge rode into the yard and dismounted. Brushing the dust from his long black coat, he came across the yard straight toward the barn. I burrowed down into the hay. Then I heard his voice.

"Jeffrey Taylor."

I lay still, holding my breath.

"Jeff." He was not calling, not asking; he was saying, his voice stern.

To myself I muttered, "Damn." Then, softly aloud, just enough for him to hear: "Yes sir?"

"Come down here."

I crawled to the edge of the loft and peered down. He was standing in the doorway, his shadow rolled out before him.

He was looking up at me, his face stern and severe beneath the small black derby.

"Do you want to see me, Judge?" I asked.

"If your name is Jeff Taylor."

I climbed down, taking careful backward steps. At the foot of the ladder I let go and turned around. He walked toward me, his eyes severe.

"You're very fond of your Uncle Clay, aren't you?"

"Yes sir," I said.

"You would go to any lengths to help him, wouldn't you?"

"I would try to help any innocent man."

"Where is your uncle's horse?"

"It's gone. It must've run away."

"Yes, that's true. And with your uncle sitting on its back. Where were you last night?"

"Here."

"Do you know that two army officers came to Capstone this morning to arrest your uncle?"

"Not arrest him," I said. "Save him. He's doing secret work for them. The fools in this town—"

"Nevertheless. He's gone now. Do you know where?"

"No."

"Perhaps I do. He has some very strange friends."

"I didn't do anything," I said. "His pistols are still here. Ask Pa. Would I have forgot them if I was going to help him?"

The Judge nodded. "Not only all the rest, but now a lie too."

They said that no one could ever tell the Judge a successful lie, but that didn't stop people from trying I guess.

"I spoke to your father this morning," the Judge said. "He said you weren't here last night."

"I was walking in the road," I said, looking the Judge in the eye. "If I was going to help Uncle Clay, wouldn't I have given him the pistols? He couldn't get far without them."

"He had a pistol," the Judge said.

"The horse must have run to him," I said. Once you start to tell a lie it's like rolling down a hill; you can't stop and you can't do anything but go faster. "And Uncle Clay probably had the extra pistol in his saddlebag."

"And the horse, I suppose, handed it to him through the bars?"

I looked at the Judge, my mouth hung open for the moment, then I looked away, ashamed, but not because I had helped Uncle Clay but because I was making such a poor job now of covering it.

"You've broken the law," the Judge said. "You and that hellion Pete Mariah."

"Pete?" I said.

"Yes. And worse than that, you let your uncle ride off before he could be adjudged innocent or guilty. Now everyone has made up their minds and it looks worse for him than ever. Do you realize what you've done?" he said, his voice suddenly angry, like I'd never heard it before. "Do you realize what you've meddled in? This is no child's play." Now he lifted his arm and held it off away from him to point at something that was invisible but symbolically present. "Do you realize what's going on down there? That this is a war that threatens the very survival of our country?"

I guess I knew that. I hadn't thought of it much, but I knew it.

He brought his arm down and took a step closer. I wasn't afraid but I felt a trifle ashamed. It was a peculiarly uncomfortable feeling.

"You think those men wanted to hang your Uncle Clay because he was swift with their women once upon a time, eh?" he said. "Then you don't seem to know anything at all. You think that twenty or thirty honest God-fearing men would come together here for that?"

"They never liked him," I said, offering feeble rebuttal.

"But always tolerated him. But now they suspect him of selling out his country for whatever cash money he can get for it."

"It's not true," I said stubbornly.

"You're the high judge of that, aren't you? You could well go to jail for what you did. And if it's proven that your uncle is a traitor then you could be hung. You have no idea of what you've turned loose. He might well be the cause of death for thousands of our soldiers—for some of the very friends and neighbors you saw volunteer and march away to war."

I was going to say, *Maybe he has some good and profound reason for doing it,* but I didn't say it, didn't want to, didn't want to hear the sound of it because I didn't want it to be true. I had a cold moment of fear thinking that perhaps it could be true, but I rejected it immediately and found myself bristling with self-reproach for admitting any such possibility, and resentment toward the Judge for provoking it.

"He'll prove you're all wrong, you'll see," I said. "When the war is over."

The Judge gazed at me. "All right, Jeff," he said sadly. He turned and started to leave and I was wondering how he knew about Pete when he stopped in the doorway and looked back at me. "I know about the pistol too," he said. "Old Clint Peady sneezed out his story this morning. Said it was five Copperheads, all over six feet tall."

CHAPTER 4

1

That was the summer. Then the autumn stains were upon the land, blooding the woods. Dying leaves filled the windy skies and rolled along the road and piled in whispering heaps against the stone walls as the wind pulled colder and stronger out of the north.

Pa and I were in the yard piling wood. We had put up several cords when Pa stopped, not suddenly but slowly. He was looking behind the house toward the pasture where two people were walking. The sun was behind them and for a moment I couldn't tell who they were. I shaded my eyes and saw. It was Rachel, walking with George Adamson.

"What is this?" Pa said. He walked several paces and then stopped, his arms at his sides. The two figures in the pasture parted. Adamson took the side path through the woods, Rachel came on alone, walking dreamily, her yellow hair bright and firelike in the sun. Pa waited, his eyes fixed upon her small and furious. She came up from the pasture, walking on the dry grass, past the barn and into the yard.

She was watching Pa, not defiantly, not even expectantly, but with some manner of strong, mobilizing pride.

"Do you know what you are doing?" Pa asked her when she got close enough for us to hear her steps.

"I've done nothing," she said to him across the yard, coming nearer.

They didn't speak again until they were facing each other.

"You walk with him," Pa said, "after what his father tried to do to your uncle?"

"It has nothing to do with him. He's been away to school. He probably doesn't even know about it."

"He knows. His father probably sent him here to spy, to try and find out where your uncle has gone."

"We never mentioned Clay."

"No? Then what were you doing, out there alone with him?"

"What are you implying?"

"Answer me," Pa said. He took her by the wrist.

"We were walking and talking."

"I don't want you to see an Adamson. Never. Do you hear?"

"What his father is has nothing to do with him."

"If I see him here again I'll take after him with a rifle. I'll show him all the feeling his father tried to show your uncle."

She pulled her hand free, her mouth pressing in for a moment until her hand was away. She walked toward the house. Pa watched her, his short, dogged body stiff with anger. Then he looked at me.

"George Adamson," he said.

I'd never liked George Adamson anyway, even without counting his father. He was an annoyingly reticent person, not shy and not supercilious, but somewhere between, who was several years older than I, but whom I had never seen on a horse or with a rifle, whom his father had sent to schools in New England and probably because he was not proud of George and preferred to have him elsewhere.

Now he was home again, walking around in fancy clothes with a book under his arm, tipping his hat to the ladies the same as the Reverend did, and all the ladies fond of him the way they will be about young men who don't spit or wear hardworn clothes.

He had a way of looking at you from right under his eyelids and a smile on his lips, only it wasn't a smile but the way his mouth was, as if he was about to smile or was trying to keep from it, which could be considerably puzzling to some of those unsophisticated farmers we had around Capstone. When he spoke (which was infrequently enough to be annoying) he had a way of nodding and then lifting his head back and appraising you with those superior eyes which lay back under thin, white brows that looked as if they were pasted on.

Rachel wouldn't talk to Pa about it and Pa went on brooding, walking off into the sunrise every morning to begin his day, Tom and I following. Adamson didn't show on the farm again after that first time, which was a good thing because Pa was in a bad frame of mind what with people still vexed about Uncle Clay's escape (The Judge was the only one who seemed to have figured it out.) and still saying that Uncle Clay was working for the Confederate Government and no letter or word from or about him as the weeks passed and all the leaves fell and you could feel winter's first silvery chill in the air and the ground turning hard. Pa knew she was riding out somewhere in the afternoons; he'd come in from the pasture and she wouldn't be there and neither would lunch and sometimes not even dinner and her horse not in the stable.

In some ways we were quite close, Rachel and I, close in that we had an instinct for the other's thought. She never tried to play mother to me, not overtly, but it was all there, gentle and subtle: the meals and the laundered things and warm sheets on my bed on a cold night and an ability (and willingness) to draw me out when there was a cloud on my brow; but never the hovering solicitation of the real mother, not the righteousness or the crooning or the lament. We seldom confided, openly, to each other, because we really didn't have to, because we had that ineffable instinct for the other's thought. So I didn't question her about George Adamson. I didn't have to, because I knew. He meant nothing to her. She was seeing him because she was lonely and because life was beginning to disappoint her. But Pa didn't, couldn't, know this, because he was too stubborn and too bitter to unbend even an inch. So she let him go on thinking what he might. And she went on seeing Adamson, even though she probably hated him. And I knew, I knew as sure as God had put that terrible maple in front of our house, that there was going to be trouble from it.

2

It was the first time Doctor Granberry had been in the house since Ma died. I could feel him upstairs, feel his presence, the same as I could feel a cloud that passes in front of the sun—his grave thoughtfulness and deliberation, everything being duly pondered, word and thought and gesture. Nothing brisk or quick about him. So I could feel him there, and it was as if he might stay up there for a year and that I would sit still until he came down.

Pa was sitting by the cold hearth. The streaks in his beard were the same color as the dead ashes in the hearth. I still had on my boots. They were the first things I had put on when Pa had thrown open my door and broken my sleep with telling me to ride for the doctor, not saying for who or why and I not asking; and I had ridden fast—untucked and unbuttoned and wild-haired—through the dead cold compact darkness to Doctor Granberry's house where there always was a lantern burning on the porch if he was in; and he had ridden back after me, loud and steady, perhaps peeved because I wouldn't let his horse catch mine until we had pulled up in the yard.

Tom was sitting on the bottom step, still in his drawers, the sleep not quite out of his stunned face, his eyes watching us as if waiting for the explanation, or perhaps pitying us because we were older and more in pain because we understood it more fully.

I heard the door open, then close. The doctor came down the stairs slowly, heavily, as if bearing the burden of all the ills he had seen. When I looked at him, the shadows lifting hugely from him as he reached the bottom step telling Tom not to move, he was yawning widely, his mouth looking as though it were about to shout but had forgotten what. He was a large, lumpy man who walked with a forward bent, his white hair uncombed, in various starts and thrusts. He came to Pa, to the cold hearth, and stood with his bag in his hand, gazing into the cold, ashy, unfired hearth.

"I guess you suspect the nature of it, Adam," he said.

"I am not a physician," Pa said.

The doctor looked at him, his eyes sharp inside of thick white eyebrows. Pa sat still, his head bent, his eyes gazing soberly into the hearth, his breathing ruffling his beard.

"She's with child," the doctor said quietly, not regretfully, merely saying it.

"Yes," Pa said.

The doctor shifted his bag from one hand to the other. I walked with him out to the porch. We stood on the top step before the chilled, soundless night. The leafless trees were beginning to stiffen in the settling cold, like corpses. Above the trees the stars lay fixed, watchful, as if meditating coldly the tides of the earth.

"Did she say anything?" I asked.

"No," the doctor said.

"You didn't ask her?"

He looked at me now, curiously, coolly, the same as the stars were watching the vigorous ceaseless follies below their ken.

"No sir," he said. "I did not."

"But don't we have to know?"

"We do not."

"Pa knows. Adamson had better go back to his school."

"Yes," the doctor said. "We're going to have more trouble now, aren't we?"

"Trouble makes trouble," I said. "One leads into the next. It can go on forever."

"Well I can't say anything about that," he said, sighing, beginning to go down the steps, slowly, with a certain oldness that defies and dispirits, gives a disconcerting sense of pupilage. He went toward the stable, very slow in the dark, very old.

3

The trouble began two nights later, on a day whose black clouds seemed to have been portending since gray morning, gathering and darkening, hovering low and close upon the treetops like things intersecting the domains of earth and sky, absorbing in their thick soft masses all of light. Then a hard wind began, cold and alien, surging through the billowing clouds, churning them until they began to seethe and a rumbling thunder spoke from afar. When the legitimate night came the thunder was still rumbling deep and sullen in the leaden clouds, carried along by the rain-smelling wind, illuminated grotesquely by frenetic flashes of lightning.

For two days Pa had not spoken. During the day he wandered about the fields, not working, walking with his head down and his eyes fast upon the ground, absorbing winter's bleak, flinty mood. At night he sat with the same brooding fastness before the fire, staring at the fire as though trying to reduce it to some mathematical formula. Then the night of the second day, with the storm rapidly building with headstrong maturity outside, with the shuddering sounds of a terrific slashing combat in the yard between the wind and the maple (with the treetop whirling and scattering its leaves like flocks of frenzied birds but otherwise making no concession to the storming wind, answering it from a throat similarly primeval and towering and indomitable, locked in gargantuan combat), Pa suddenly kicked out at the row of pokers, some of them toppling and striking sparky red blows upon the fire, the others clanging to the stone base. He rose, turning to me.

"It cannot go unpunished," he said. He looked up toward the head of the stairs at Rachel's door. "She sits there, unconcerned, swelling with an illicit life; and he sits where he is, smug and amused as if there are no engines of retribution upon this earth."

"She's not unconcerned," I said. "She's sick about it."

"Which hardly absolves the fact," he said, his eyes still raised, fixed upon the closed door where the shadows from the upstairs candle flickered slowly.

"What are you going to do?" I asked.

"Go to your room," he said.

"I don't think I ought to," I said.

But he was so possessed by the wrath and passion of his course that my defiance went unnoticed. He started toward the stairs. I followed. We went up together. I kept staring at his face which was set as if he were glimpsing at eternity, his head held up with blind, dangerous righteousness, totally unmindful of me. When we reached her door he paused for a moment, setting himself to slay some pagan deity, his eyes

hardened to gaze upon blood and death. I raised my hand.
"Pa," I said.

He smashed open the door with his foot. The wind tore into us through the open window, roaring in the dark room like a lair of beasts, the white curtains streaming and snapping and billowing. She was sitting there with flying hair, her face turned toward us. He went straight toward her and I thought he would say something first but he never spoke. He took her by the arm and jerked her to her feet. She stared at him, her eyes amazed and afraid but still proud. Then he jerked her forward with such force she fell to the floor. Still he did not relinquish her arm, beginning to drag her. I tried to break the grip, and I did, for a moment, but he immediately restored it, taking her by the hand this time, with his other hand striking me in the face, stunning me. She began to scream. He dragged her across the floor and through the door, his short dogged body leaned forward as if dragging some unwieldy sack. I ran at him again, trying to part their hands but his grip was iron. She had stopped struggling, stopped screaming, lying there in her twisted dress. He let go her hand. He looked at me, fierce and severe behind the beard, alien, not my father, not any man, not anyone.

"Go to your room," he said.

"What are you going to do?" I asked.

"Go to your room," he said again, his breath running short, impatient, "or by the Lord Jesus I'll lay a whip to you!" And to Rachel: "Get to your feet." Slowly she rose, sobbing, her hair littered over her eyes, her dress dirty and twisted.

"Go downstairs," he said.

I watched, leaning over the bannister, Tom behind me

now, out from our room, shivering with fear. They went down the stairs, slowly, silently, their shadows descending the wall like tall black flowers. He had her hand again but now she was not resisting. Her head was bowed. She seemed to have seen the mark of her fate and was moving upon it devoid of despair, all hope washed from her as though by an ocean. I watched as the wind poured at my back and pounded the rafters, whisking to extinction the upstairs candle. They walked before the fire, she still led by the hand, then past the fire, and she was sobbing pitifully now and I wondered why she was permitting it, what desperate penance was guiding her. They passed beneath the chandelier and then were gone from sight but when a moment later the wind and the thunder became louder I knew they had gone out, the door banging back wind-struck. I ran downstairs, running toward the storming night but suddenly he appeared in the doorway, his eyes glaring, his beard whipping in the wind, and hit me in the face and I went down, my legs gone from under me and then jerking up before my eyes. Then he was gone and the night was roaring in the empty doorway, demoniac, screaming, and I could hear the tree snarling and hissing like some clawing dragon, slashed by the wind, threatened by the grotesque veins of lightning and the booming collapses of thunder, all its boughs heaving and snarling as the wind like the wild ghost of some ancient sea kept hurling upon it in slashing tides.

As I got to my feet the rain began, became immediately a wild teeming curtain, rattling over the porch like thousands of scurrying feet. I went to the doorway. I couldn't see them. I didn't know where they had gone. The tree sounded now like the ghost-waters were caught in the whirling branches, there was a great surflike roaring all through the night. The wind drove the rain into my face and I stepped back for a moment and in that moment the lightning opened the night with a horrible splitting and macabre dance of white glare that silverized the dashing rain and revealed a terrifying scene. I saw in the glare—it was merely for a split second—Pa bent at the tree, binding Rachel's half-collapsed body to the trunk, the rope around her breasts and her legs, her hair blown around half covering her face like something leaping for a moment out of a tableau of medieval witchcraft. Then it was gone, as quickly as it had appeared, and I was running down the porch and across the yard, through the sweeping sheets of rain. Pa suddenly loomed up out of it, stopping me.

"What are you doing?" I cried.

"Get back to the house!" he commanded.

I tried to get to Rachel but I couldn't get by him. I could see her bound against the tree, struggling helplessly in all the sweep and noise and roar. The lightning came again and she screamed at it, the thunder crashing upon her voice as again and again the blasts of wind tore into the roaring tree, flinging the rain torrents through the night. I fought with him but his strength was too great. I fell to the loud streaming earth, the rain suddenly swarming noisily around me, into my face. He yanked me to my feet. "You can't!" I shouted into his maddened face. He pushed me back toward the house. I saw her again in another flash of lightning, tied to the tree, struggling desperately now with the ropes as if being strangled, her contorted face lifted to the swooping thrusting branches, and when the thunder had crashed again heard her screaming, not loud but desperate, terrified, entreating.

All that night I listened to the rain and thunder, and to the tree; lying on the bed in the locked room, cold and shivering, being awakened from time to time by the sudden entrance of shuddering silver flashes, Tom lying next to me asking over and over: "Why is she out there, Jeff? Why? Why?"

I watched from the window early the next morning when he cut her free. It was a gray, somber day, everything wet and gray and leaden, a canopy of gloom low upon everything, as if the earth were morosely resentful of the terrible lashing it had taken the night before. In the yard were black puddles, fallen leaves wet-pasted everywhere. It looked as if it might begin to rain again, but it didn't. The day just hung like that, gray and somber and spent, like something born out of its time.

She was unconscious. When I had risen, just after the wind had stopped and then the rain too, she had been hanging limply forward in the ropes like a broken flower, her head hung forward, her yellow hair streaming down. One large branch had been torn from the tree and lay near her, battered and lifeless. The wind had torn her dress in several places and I could see the pinkness of her neck and part of her shoulder.

I would have broken down the door then to get to her, but just then he appeared, walking out from beneath the eaves, walking across the yard with a knife in his hand. Coming up to her he stopped and stared for a moment. Then he kneeled and began sawing at the ropes around her legs, then at the others. He caught her over his arm as, the ropes collapsing around her, she fell forward, still unconscious, like something stuffed with rags and sawdust. Putting the knife into his belt, he picked her up and carried her in his arms, walking back across the yard, his head held back, grim and indomitable, splashing through the puddles; walking slowly, with slow short dogged steps, Rachel's head lolling from side to side like a sleeping child's, her feet swinging. Then they disappeared under the eaves and I could hear him on the porch, his feet clumping, then coming into the house, walking downstairs; then coming up the stairs, slow and heavy with his burden (I was standing at the door then, listening, my ear pressed to it), going into Rachel's room, the door slamming loudly, the sound of a key locking it a moment later: and then Pa coming down the hall and unlocking our door, walking away as I opened it, not saying anything, going down the stairs, his thick galluses making a white X across the back of his blue shirt.

For the next five days I didn't see her. Pa wouldn't let us into the room. It was always locked. He would bring her meals up and then carry out the dishes (most of the time the food had not even been touched) and lock the door again and go back downstairs.

"Why don't you let her come out?" I asked.

"She doesn't want to," he said. "It's not on her mind just now."

"Then why do you keep the door locked?"

He didn't answer.

Once, passing the door, I stopped and laid my ear against it. I heard her in there making faint little sounds, like moaning, like the wind on a freezing night. When I whispered her name the sounds stopped. I stood by the door for a long time and as long as I stood there the room remained quiet.

At night I could hear her. She would be talking to herself. I could hear her voice, low and thin, murmuring words that I could not quite distinguish, that did not sound quite coherent and at first I thought she was talking in her sleep but then I knew it wasn't that, because it happened the first night and then the second and the third, carrying on all night sometimes, the voice going on and on, like someone ill with fever. In the mornings when I crossed the yard to go to the fields I would look up at the window but she was never there and the window looked so very strange and empty and forlorn. One night there was a scream. It shattered my sleep and the next thing I knew I had leaped out of bed and was standing barefoot on the cold floor just beginning to come out of my sleep, feeling it flowing out of me in a hot, dizzying wave, like some wooly garment departing my soul; the scream gone but its sound lingering in piercing echo, freezing the night, the silence, embodying it with a shivering tension, a stifling abeyant imminence.

"It was Rachel!" Tom whispered, his eyes staring at me over the top of the covers, the rest of him burrowing underneath.

I went to the door. I heard Pa passing. I could see the thin light moving under the door as he passed with his candle. I heard him unlock the door, then close it behind him. I heard her sobbing and whimpering then. A long time of quiet, constant sobbing, and I tried to picture it, how it must be: Rachel sprawled on the bed, the grief and anguish sobbing out of her, and Pa sitting stolidly behind his candle, watching. I stood by the door for almost an hour, then went back to bed, listening to the soft sad sobbing until I fell back to sleep.

Pa remained sullenly wordless those days. I found it impossible to speak to him, he was unapproachable. If I had known what he was thinking, what his silence was brooding over, I could have spoken. But I didn't know. I didn't know if he was feeling remorse or guilt or some kind of puritanical high-mindedness. Nothing showed in his face.

We sat the chilly fall nights in silence, in the living room staring into the fire which Tom would lay just before supper, sat until the fire burned itself down and Pa would tell us to go upstairs to our room and then later we would hear him coming up and going to his own room.

It seemed that something new, strange, mysterious had come into the house and would remain, uncanny and irremovable. We sensed it more than knew it. It was there upon us all the time, heard but unseen, audible but not coherent, near but far, with a sense of lingering, of gathering, like age, like dust.

But we waited. Not because we were patient but because we were awed; there was fear and dread and wonder. We watched Pa, waited for it to come from him, because he knew, he was the only one who went into that room. But Pa did and said nothing, he showed nothing, and it seemed that we might have to wait forever.

Then on the morning of the sixth day George Adamson

appeared. It was just after supper and I was in the barn when I heard his horse. I went out into the yard and saw him. He was just dismounting, one leg on the ground, the other lifting out of the stirrup. He was dressed in fine black broadcloth, crowned by a small, dark derby hat. Completely dismounted, he stood and groomed himself with his hands for a moment, flicking away a thread, brushing carefully, his head bent, his chin rolled in two. I went out toward him and he stopped when he saw me, that smile that wasn't quite a smile on his lips, his eyes staring with that proud, shy reticence that I could never quite accept, eyes like a cow's, lethargic, ruminative.

"What are you doing here?" I asked. "Pa's inside. If he sees you. . . ."

"Good," he said. "I want him to see me. I want to see him."

"You must be crazy," I said.

He began walking toward the house, swinging easily, almost effeminately in his finery. I followed, staring at his tall, straight, immaculate back, thinking—I couldn't help this either—of how the dust was going to show all over that black broadcloth when Pa shot him down. But he kept going, smug and confident and imperious, as if Pa and the shotgun would mean nothing; up the porch steps, into the house. I went in after him. He looked around, removing his hat.

"You still got time to get out," I whispered.

He didn't hear though, he didn't listen.

"Is your sister at home?" he asked.

"She's not feeling so well," I said.

"Please tell your father I would like to see him. That George Adamson wishes to see him."

"Do you know what you're doing?" I asked.

"I'm quite aware."

"Do you have a pistol?"

"Why should I carry a sidearm?"

"I don't want them to say. . . ." But I didn't finish. Pa was standing there, in the doorway, short and churlish and intractable, staring at Adamson, staring as if he never expected anyone to see him there.

"It's all right, Jeff," he said. "No man who enters this house has ever to fear for his safety. It's still a Christian house, despite the wrongs and the injustices perpetrated upon it."

Adamson, holding his hat against his chest (but not humbly the way certain people, like peddlers or beggers, do, but with a sense of decorum, of propriety), took a few steps forward.

"I would like to talk to you, Mr. Taylor, about something which is of a deep personal nature to us both."

Pa came out of the doorway, one thumb hung in his suspender, his pipe in his hand.

"Go outside, Jeff," he said.

"No," I said, not stubborn or perverse, but quiet, determined. We exchanged glances. He had been telling, or indicating things to me all week that I didn't want to do but had done: I had kept away from Rachel's room, had not tried to communicate with her, had refrained from asking questions, from disputing with him. I had done all that but he saw now that I would not do this, that I would not trust the two of them alone there no matter what he said. My eyes told him that and he saw and did not press further. He looked back to Adamson.

"All right," he said. "What do you want?"

Not nervous, not revolving his hat around the way you might expect a man at such a moment to be doing, not shy or nervous or blundering, he said it quite simply, calmly, directly: "I feel I'm in love with your daughter, sir. I'm here to seek her hand in marriage."

I thought sure Pa would take out after him then, I was ready for it, I would have stopped it, used my strength against him this time. But it wasn't necessary. He didn't do anything. He just stood there, the one thumb hooked inside the suspender, the pipe smoking in the other hand, the face, the eyes calm, the beard unruffled even by breathing.

"Is that what you're here for, Mr. Adamson?" he said quietly, ironically—too much so, I thought—not as I expected him to speak, in fact not as he had ever spoken before.

"Yes sir," Adamson said. "I assure you my feelings are quite sincere, my proposal genuine. I know you probably disapprove, that there's been trouble between yourself and my father, but I do not believe that the offenses of one generation should be held against. . . ."

"Oh no," Pa said mildly, still ironic. "I bear no grudge against you. As you say, the trouble is between myself and your father." He seemed almost to be tasting his words, and the taste was bad, biting them off one at a time, quiet, restrained.

"You see, sir," Adamson went on, "I've always admired your daughter from afar. When I came home from school this time I had made up my mind. I had resolved. . . ."

"Yes," Pa said, not mildly now. "I know what you resolved. But this question should be decided by my daughter."

Adamson stood straighter, his chin lifting. He hadn't expected it to be this uncomplicated. "I have your blessings then?" he asked.

"It's not for me to bless or to forbid," Pa said. "Would you like to talk to her yourself?"

"Yes sir. Very much."

Pa turned and began going up stairs. Halfway up he turned and motioned to the uncertain Adamson. "You can come up," Pa said. Adamson followed, and I after him.

Pa waited for us at the door. A puzzled look crossed Adamson's face as Pa took out the key and with it opened the door. He pushed the door slowly open. He stood aside and showed Adamson in with his hand, then followed, and I followed Pa.

The sun poured from a cool, blue, autumn sky, flooding brightly through the window, gilding the room. The room was quite disorderly, the bed in wild dishevelment, as if it had been the plaything of beasts, the covers turned and twisted. Nothing seemed in its proper place: the chairs turned to the wall, the bureau and the dressing table askew (the bureau drawers were covered by a towel tacked over them, another towel was covering the dressing-table mirror). The room, which had always been sweet-smelling and cheerful, now had a distinct musty odor which was further heightened by a certain air of gloom and despair as if clogged lungs had been breathing and rebreathing this air for months.

Adamson looked at Pa, his knitted eyebrows intensifying the unasked question. Pa smiled. He went to the closet and pulled open the door. There was a sound of something darting behind the clothes, I saw the wardrobe rustling. Pa reached in and with his hand took hold of something and gently but firmly he brought it out.

She emerged timidly, trembling, in a feeble, faltering half-crouch, her hands up to her mouth, her eyes (which had so recently been so beautiful with the warm helplessness and giving of love) were shining with timorous fear and excitement, like a child being led before a throng. The years seemed to have climbed and swarmed upon her in a matter of days, enfeebling and intimidating her. Her hair hung loose and stringy, like an upside down mop. Her dress—it was the same she had worn the night of the storm and evidently been wearing it since—was limp and tattered and looked like old, old flesh. Her shoeless feet dragged and purred as Pa led her across the carpet, through the sun's golden derision. Her startled, child's eyes widened fearfully and gazed vaguely when they set upon Adamson and she tried to draw back into the closet; but Pa held to her arm and she pressed her hands in harder against her mouth as if trying to eat something precious out of them or to stifle a cry, her eyes becoming wilder, wilder.

Adamson—he had taken a step back when Pa had taken her from the closet—took another, sharp step back. "Rachel!" he gasped, frightened and amazed.

Pa said, a bitter smile jesting behind his beard, "I think a Christmas wedding would be just fine, don't you, Mr. Adamson?"

4

At other times she was quite rational. She would sit as she had always at the window, gazing out at the road or into the branches of the maple. Some things she would remember and know, others not. She remembered Doctor Granberry and she knew why he had been called and what was happening inside of her. She remembered the night of the storm and being bound to the tree, only she spoke of it as "My beautiful experience; my look into the face of God," as though it had been some sort of divine religious experience, a vision or a visitation, a moment of divine penance in teeming and thundering purgatory; not remembering that it had been Pa that had dragged her from the house and tied her to the tree, not even remembering that Pa had had anything to do with it at all, remembering it as if it had been God or one of the angels that had done it. But she did not remember George Adamson having come to see her.

"He said he was in love with you," I said. "He wanted to marry you."

"George?" Her eyes were pleased, were flattered, but only that, not excited or hopeful. "Sweet George," she said quietly, staring out the window. "Poor George."

"A few days ago," I said.

"I must have been asleep." She laughed lightly, to herself. "That's George for you. He didn't have the courage to say it while I was awake. Men are such cowards."

"I don't think he knows you're going to be a mother."

"Of course he doesn't," she said. "How should he?"

"Doctor Granberry said that we had no business asking questions about these things."

"That's right, Jeffrey. You must be a gentleman."

"Yes," I said. "I'll be a gentleman. But only because I know."

She smiled, shyly, as if pleased that I should be sharing her secret. She was looking at the barn. She gazed upon it for a long time, her eyes bright and lusterless like polished glass, her lips lightly together, the smile lingering, wistful.

"Jeffrey," she said softly, "where is he?"

"I don't know."

"Has there been any word?"

"No. None at all."

"Is he dead?"

"No."

"Of course not. They tried to hang him, but they couldn't. He won't ever die. He's such a beautiful man. With such soft white skin, almost like a woman's. But not shy or demure like a woman, and that is what makes him so beautiful, the way those long thin woman's fingers lay themselves on you, on your breasts and your thighs, and under your thighs. . . ."

"Does he know?"

"No," she said sadly, shaking her head, her eyes wide and vague like a child's. "He's off in the war somewhere and not knowing. When he comes back, his son will already be born."

"He'll be back soon, when it's over," I said.

"Do you think so, Jeffrey?"

I went to her at the window and put my hands on her shoulders. She looked up at me and smiled, childlike, grateful. Now I was the older, the more responsible and capable, feeling it suddenly in one of those strange, tantalizing, uneasy tremblings similar to the one I had had on the night I brought the horse and the pistol to Uncle Clay, a trembling which was in collision with another which broke from a reluctantly yielding youngness.

"Yes," she said, wistful. "He'll be back." Then she said, her voice falling even more quietly, a dark excitement filling her eyes, "Please, Jeffrey, don't let George Adamson come here again. I don't want to see him. Clay wouldn't like it."

"I'll see to it," I said, feeling in my voice the terse irony, remembering George Adamson's horror and loathing, remembering him fleeing from the room, and the rapid clumping his running feet made on the stairs, the sound of his horse galloping from the yard, the sight of him disappearing down the road, frantic, almost reckless; and Pa and I walking down the stairs from the locked door and Pa cursing bitterly, his irony gone, bitter and fuming and wrathful.

"So he's seen her, and run away from the sight and what he's done. But I know where he's run."

"How long will Rachel be like that?" I asked.

"She is doing penance. For how long it must be, I don't know. It lies in other hands. But vengeance lies in my hands."

"What good will that do? In his way he's paying too. He was in love. He wanted to marry her."

"In two months he'll forget," Pa said. "But I'll not forget. He did this to her and I'm going to use my God-given strength to see that he pays."

5

Pa still did not hold himself to blame. It was the sin, the evil, something that had descended not just upon our farm and upon Capstone but upon the whole country as well, darkening the land and blooding the rivers and hurling violent unnatural light into the skies. The earth was rebelling against the blood, the broken young bodies. Everywhere there were symptoms and symbols. Men were dying. (Two brothers from Capstone had been killed during a crossing of the Rapidan and their father had become crazed at the news and fired his barn and perished in it as the volunteer firemen vainly threw buckets of water into the red, roaring flames. And other men were coming back supported by crutches or with empty sleeves flapping, old and slow, to sit dazed and baffled and curiously tranquil and unresentful as they told their stories to the staring listening men and the sighing, sensitive women; and I listened and I listened but still I did not hear the sound of guns or the noise of armies and I didn't believe these slow, prematurely old and spiritless men —it was not like when Uncle Clay told the stories, when you could hear the men smashing through the forest and smell the gunsmoke and hear the clash of sabers and see the water running off the flanks of the horses galloping up the river banks.) So Pa dissociated himself from any culpability. He had done nothing, he believed, but serve as an ordained instrument of retribution. And it was not over yet. The real punishment still awaited the co-conspirator of the sin.

I rode over to the Judge's house one evening several days later. The Judge owned the most beautiful house in Capstone, at the upper end of Grant Avenue. It was a white house with a pillared porch, the white pillars wrapped over with dark green ivy. The house was not large but it exuded a gentility and stateliness worthy of its occupant. It was set in from the Avenue behind a flat green lawn, shaded by the melancholy dignity of a large willow.

Dismounting, I went up the walk, mounted the porch and,

after pausing to beat the dust from my shirt and trousers, took the brass knocker in my hand and struck twice on the metal plate. The Judge himself answered. I had interrupted the last moments of his dinner, he was wiping a napkin across his lips.

"Can I speak to you?" I asked.

"Certainly, Jeffrey," he said. He opened the door wide and I went in. It was the first time I'd ever been inside the Judge's house and I'd never seen rugs like that before, or such chandeliers, or such enormous paintings, or such brightly polished furniture, or, when he showed me into his study, such an amount of books, from floor to ceiling you couldn't see the wall. When we sat, on opposite sides of his desk, the Judge looked at me, his sharp, sternly handsome features grave and concerned, the bright, sharp blue eyes watching me intently, bright and sharp and intent with patience and a willingness to listen and to help; and, too, a certain severity in those eyes which were not forgetting that I had been the one who had executed Uncle Clay's escape.

"It's about a lot of people," I said. "Pa, and Rachel, and George Adamson, and Uncle Clay. Pa's got it in for the Adamsons anyway, and now, soon, he's going to take after George with a shotgun for what he thinks George did to Rachel."

"Your Pa thinks that young Adamson did it?" the Judge asked with mild surprise, his eyes seeming to move a little more closely together.

"Yes sir. And he's going to take the shotgun off the wall soon enough. I can tell by the way he stops right in the middle of his work sometimes and just looks straight ahead, and the way he sits in front of the fire at night. It's as if he's timing it, just waiting, like a cat in a corner. I don't want to see Pa in trouble. That's why I've got to find Uncle Clay."

The Judge nodded. He knew then, he understood. "And you want me to tell you where he is. Well I don't know where he is, Jeff."

"You mentioned, that time in the barn, that you knew some of his friends. If I could talk to some of them—"

The Judge leaned toward me, resting his elbows on the desk. "Do you know who his friends are?" he said, a stern note of advice and forewarning in his voice, his eyes appraising me now, as if trying to measure and determine the extent of the man that would have to come from the boy. "His friends are the worst elements in Shantytown. The lowliest scum. Thieves and murderers and grave robbers and drunkards and bounty jumpers and Copperheads and. . . ."

"I don't care," I said. "If they know where he's gone, then I've got to talk to them."

CHAPTER 5

Shantytown was huddled down near the headwaters of Newtown Creek. It appeared to have grown out of some suffering, festering place. Its inhabitants were the wretchedly poor, the itinerant laborers, the miscreants and the lawless, most of them from across the river from Manhattan's crowded slums. For a while it had been the sanctuary of the old Greb gang which had ridden and plundered and murdered along the back roads from the creek to Montauk before the war until the Capstone men, led by the Judge (who had been just a lawyer then; but people had been so impressed by his daring and courage that they decided he was the man for the judgeship then vacant), had come down and put an end to them. The Reverend once called it the place where the excrement went. And if that were true then you smelled it the moment you rode into Shantytown's proximity, and smelled it more once you got into the dusty, pitted, garbage-strewn streets that wound crookedly around the shanties. Most of the shanties were nailed together with rough, irregular boards and in the walls of every dwelling were places where the disparate boards did not come together, leaving gaps and openings, some of which had been filled in with mud. Each shanty had a rusted stovepipe slanting rakishly out of its roof, puffing smoke at the sky, and most had torn potato or flour sacks hanging over the windows.

Some of the dwellings were built on little rises and these had skeletal ladders reaching down from the stepless front entrances. Most of the shanties were unbearably close together and how people could live in such close proximity bewildered me—their washlines crossing, their odors and their voices mixing. Some few of the dwellings had been whitewashed, none painted. Here and there someone had tried to cultivate a garden, but it was hopeless, for children and animals too—I saw horses and mules and pigs and scrawny gawking roosters—ran and scratched and gabbled everywhere. Garbage was strewn all around, sometimes in great heaps, rotting malodorously in the sun, buzzing with clouds of black flies. Pieces of rough-hewn timber and sawed tree trunks lay all around, much of it partially burnt. The outbuildings leaned drunkenly on one another.

The people were a sullen, suspicious lot. They stared wordlessly as I rode by—women pausing at their washing, children at their play, men in their squatting conversation taking hard looks at me from under their caps and derbies.

Nearby the creek flowed. It was very dirty here; from here it carried garbage and refuse and burnt logs and empty rum barrels and more than occasionally a battered corpse. The waters were valiantly swift and bright in the sun, reflecting the light-enriched clouds. I rode along the bank, past a group of small, dirty-faced boys who looked up at me as if saluting, their hands against their brows to cover their eyes from the sun. Up ahead were several stores, standing in a row, all of them shaded by slanting wooden awnings, risen on wooden sidewalks. Two of them were saloons, and there was a barbershop (a man was sitting outside on a barrel, arms crossed, head bent, getting his hair cut) and a grocer's, and, further down, a smith. A dead dog lay in the street, a cloud of green flies busy on a red wound in its underside, the flies lifting and scattering for a moment as I rode by. A man selling brooms was walking along the side of the road, his wares mounted across his shoulder like so many effeminate rifles, his high hat covered with dust. Several youths looked up at me from carving the earth with penknives, their faces thin and hard and inscrutable, their mouths tersely speechless, inarticulate. A woman carrying a bucket of water up from the creek trudged by, her hair hanging in strings over her bent shoulders, her eyes glancing up at me for a moment from brooding depths; and I wondered if she might be one of the women that Pete Mariah came down here to see, the kind that he would talk about late into the night while lying on his back in the grass shooting smoke streams up at the stars, and telling me that it was damned people with unrequited love who said that the moon and the stars and the night sounds were lonely and melancholy.

Three men stumbled out of one of the saloons, one of them toppling off the wooden sidewalk and landing on his back in the road, his derby rolling away. His friends stuck out their chests and laughed coarsely at him. Shakily and tenaciously he made his way back onto his feet again, looking around for his hat, only to collapse again, thudding into the road amid a cloud of dust as his friends regaled themselves with laughter, holding onto the wooden post to prevent their own collapse as the one in the road struggled woozily to rise again, mouthing vague, incoherent curses. I reined in and dismounted and went to him and took him under the arms and raised him, putting my knee into his rump to get him up straight.

"If he's your friend," I said to the other two, "you'll help him to stand." They stopped laughing and looked at me, perhaps resentful, perhaps with mortification. One stepped down and took my charge from me, holding him steady, staring at him with flat, dry, colorless eyes that resembled congealed raindrops.

"Say now, Dan," he said to the helpless one, "this won't do at all."

The helpless one half turned to me, his eyes astonishingly blue and clear in his bearded face.

"Bless your belly, lad," he said.

They sat him down on the boardwalk and he hung his head. I put his hat down next to him.

The Judge had given me the name of Alamine Johnson. This, he said, was one of Uncle Clay's friends. (And he had said it with baffled regret.)

"Maybe one of you can help me," I said. "I'm looking for a gentleman named Alamine Johnson."

"Gentleman you say?" one of them said and went off into a roar of laughter that twisted him around so that he had to grab hold of the post to stop from collapsing into the street. The helpless one raised his head and stared at me, coolly, steadily, his eyes not at all like the rest of him, not trembling and hopeless and prideless.

"What would you want with him, lad?" he asked.

"I have to talk to him—personal," I said.

"Are you sure he's the one you're after?"

"His name was given to me."

"By who?"

"Someone."

The man sighed, scratching at his beard, making a sound like walking on dried straw.

"He's inside," he said, thumbing over his shoulder. "In this place here. Does he want to see you, lad?"

"He doesn't know me. But he knows my uncle."

The man shrugged, taking his hand away from his beard. I tied my horse to the post and stepped up onto the sidewalk and went into the saloon, leaving my three friends outside, the one still hanging on to the post, another just standing stupified waiting for some shock or reflex to tumble him into the street, and the other sitting headbent contemplating clasped hands.

It was like stepping into a cave; there was that same gloomy presence of time spent and withered, of treachery and brooding oblivion. It was unlike any saloon I had ever seen before. The bar consisted of a long plank supported by three sturdy barrels standing about eight feet apart. Behind it a man in a long, black apron—the kind that Bumper Clark wore while working over his anvil—was serving drinks to several men, taking the bottles from a shelved packing crate behind him. The roof had a leaden sag in its middle and probably would have collapsed if not for the scarred wooden post that braced it. There were no windows and the fetid air seemed to hang in windless suspension, like a gray veil, the foul odors and breathings clinging to it, and I felt as if an ignited match held aloft would burn it all away and reveal latent daylight, brightness.

Opposite the improvised bar were several tables and chairs. Sitting at one of the tables was a man, a stranger to me, at once imposing and intimidating. He was watching me, and had evidently been watching me from the moment I walked through the door. His head, chest and shoulders were massive. He had a short, fierce, black beard which with his short side whiskers shaped a black frame for his face out of which bulged a thick round nose. A drooping black mustache hid his mouth. His large, deep eyes watched me with willful, calculated hostility. I paused for a moment, sensing that this was the man I was looking for. I went to the table, looking back into his eyes now which continued to follow my every move, staring now with crude, thick curiosity.

"I'm looking for a Mr. Alamine Johnson," I said.

But for a moment it was as if I had yet to speak. The watchful eyes did not even blink. Carefully, fronting some depth of massive ponderous concentration, they remained upon my face. Then he nodded. His moist red lips moved in the beard. "Sit down," he said.

I sat across from him. A whiskey bottle and a glass stood before him.

"My name is Jeff Taylor," I said. "Clay Taylor is my uncle."

"And my friend," he said.

"Yes. I know."

"How do you know?"

"Someone told me. I had to find somebody who knows where Uncle Clay went."

"Clay stopped off here the night he busted jail," Johnson said. "He didn't have much time, of course. We talked a little, killed a bottle, and he went on."

"Do you know where?"

He paused. We peered across the table into each other's eyes. And eyes were about all that showed of his face, what with his beard and mustache and the thick black hair covering most of his forehead; but yet he was still a young man, with the thick nose that somehow impressed me as being the source of terrific and violent strength; probably the same age as Uncle Clay and toward this fact I accounted for their friendship, that it was the similarity of their years that had brought them together and no other reason, because the Judge had warned gravely that Alamine Johnson was one of the most unsavory men in Shantytown, a drunkard, a thief, a moral snake, and probably even a Copperhead too (this last because once, in the spring, a barge coming down the creek loaded with material headed for the government ships in the Hudson River had been boarded while passing Shantytown and fired and sunk, and the description of the leader of the invaders as given by the barge's captain had fitted Alamine Johnson who, when the police and government officials had come to Shantytown to question him, had suddenly disappeared, not reappearing until five weeks later). Now he asked,

"Are you the nephew who helped him bust jail?"

"Yes," I said, feeling a sudden warm pride, for Uncle

Clay had spoken of me, and well too—I could see that now in this man's face, in a barely perceptible softening there, a relaxation of the suspicion and hostility in his eyes.

"Will you have some whiskey?" he asked.

"No thank you," I said, regretting it the moment I did. "The reason I came down here was to ask you if you could tell me where my uncle is."

"Why?"

"It's personal—real personal. But important, just as important as it could be."

"You might as well ask where the wind is," he said. He poured himself another glassful, but did not touch it.

"But you must have some idea. You say he was here, that you talked."

"I have an idea." He lifted the glass and with puckered lips drank. When he put the glass down his eyes were shut; when they opened they were watching me, thoughtfully now, pondering, as if trying to determine how important this was to Uncle Clay.

"How do you know he wants you poking around after him down there?"

"I told you," I said. "It's as important as it can be."

"I don't know how important that is."

"Two lives depend on it. One of them my father's, his brother. He's got to hear what I have to tell him."

He pondered again. He wasn't happy about this, I could tell. He was measuring the responsibility of telling me against the confidence Uncle Clay had placed in him.

"Well, I don't know where he is, but there's certain places he turns up at from time to time. One is a place called Baker

Station in northern Virginia. It's just the other side of the Potomac. But it's hardly a place for a youth to go riding nowadays. Very unhealthy place just now."

"I don't care," I said.

"You might not even get through. Chances are the Army would chase you right back if they caught you. Then there's a lot of Rebel cavalry that swings through there."

"I'll be careful. I know how to ride. And I know how to take care of myself. When I get to Baker Station how do I go about finding him?"

"There's an inn there, Blackhurst's by name. Clay goes there for two- or three-day spells when he's in the neighborhood. You go there and ask for him. If he's just been there then you may as well turn around and come back because it's usually a couple months before he turns up again."

"How do you know he goes there?"

"I know what I know," Johnson said. "And maybe I shouldn't even have told you this much."

"It's all right. You don't have to worry. I know Uncle Clay is doing secret work. . . ."

"You do?"

"Yes. I guess you know it too. The people in Capstone think he's riding dispatches for the South, but he told me different, only it can't be let out till the war's over."

"That's right," Johnson said.

"Have you ever been down there, to Baker Station?"

"Before the war. My advice to you is to keep off the main roads, and if you get caught not to say who you're looking for. Tell them you want to join up. They'll chase you back then."

"I'd join up, if they'd let me," I said.

He shrugged, drinking again.

"I want to thank you," I said.

"For Clay Taylor's nephew, especially for the one who sprung him from jail—why not? You sure you won't take a whiskey?" he asked.

"I'd be proud to drink with you," I said.

He poured into his glass, about three fingers' worth, as I watched, bracing myself, wetting my underlip. I lifted to him and drank it down at a single gulp. I felt my face turning hot and my insides felt as if they were going to blow out. I turned away, almost choking on the cough that I refused to let come. Johnson smiled. I got up. He wasn't watching me now.

"Good-by," I said.

"Good luck to you," he said. "And if you do see Clay down there, tell him Alamine Johnson says to take care."

All the way back up Grant Avenue I kept feeling as though that whiskey was going to rise up and throw me right out of the saddle, and I kept cursing myself over and over for having let Alamine Johnson see that it had been the first time I'd ever taken a whiskey.

2

That night I found Uncle Clay's pistols. Pa had hidden them in his room and since the door there was always locked these days (because he had hid the pistols in there, probably), I had to climb up onto the eaves and from there get into the room. It was taking a chance because Pa was downstairs, but it had been taking a chance to get Clint Peady's pistol the way we did and bring it and the horse to Uncle Clay and had been taking a chance riding down to Shantytown like that; so I took it because I had to and because I was not afraid.

He had them hid in the back of the top shelf in the closet, wrapped around in one of Uncle Clay's sweaters. I took the pistols and tucked them into my belt and climbed back down again and went across the yard and hid them in the stable. Then I went back to the house and into the living room and stood near the fire, watching Pa from the corner of my eye. He was slumped deep in his chair, Ma's old red shawl around his shoulders, gazing quietly upon the fire, a strange, deep melancholy in his face and I knew he was thinking of Ma. Tom was already asleep upstairs. Rachel's room was quiet; it seemed now as if the quiet had come to stay in that room. Already I had begun to be accustomed to it, to not seeing her, and it bothered me and I tried to fight it but it kept growing on me; but it seemed, since that last time I had seen her, that it was not Rachel there in that room in that mysterious and suspended silence any longer, but some stranger, some new person who looked like Rachel and who wore her clothes but whose inside was not Rachel. But I would dream about her sometimes and it would make me feel better, because I did not want to abandon her, and would not abandon her even if I was growing up so fast, becoming full a man so fast (even if I did almost choke on Alamine Johnson's whiskey) that everything that had ever happened before was like summer's colors vanishing swift and unmourned before autumn's chilly heralding.

Pa looked so very old and sad and alone now, sitting with

his sorrow and his hate and his smoldering furnace of vengeance. The red fire reflected like a pale flush on his face. He looked like the kind of man you bypass on tiptoe with private, unstated compassion because words of consolation would be futile and satiric. But I had to say it anyway because tomorrow morning I was going to begin.

"I have to say something," I said. "About Adamson."

"Adamson?" he asked, asking it in that wary inquiring way because there were two Adamsons that he hated, and I knew that.

"Yes. Not one or the other, but the name. I want to know if that is what's bothering you. Are you going to kill him because of what his father tried to do, or because of what you think he did?"

Pa raised his head and looked up at me. "Think? Think?" he said sharply. "Ask Doctor Granberry what I 'think'."

"I'm not doubting the doctor. I just don't want you committing a murder."

"You're interfering again, Jeffrey," he said, saying it quietly, almost mildly, conversationally.

"No. This time I'm participating. If you kill George Adamson you'll not only be committing murder, but committing it upon the wrong man—unless it really makes no difference to you, that you don't care who or what you're shooting at as long as its name is Adamson."

"The wrong man?" he asked, his eyes fixed upon me. He didn't seem to have listened to any of the rest of it, only that—the wrong man.

"George Adamson is not the one."

"How do you know this?"

"Because I know who did it."

"Who?"

"I can't tell you. He's not in Capstone now. But tomorrow morning I'm leaving. I'm going to bring him back."

He continued to look up at me, amazed and baffled, his upturned face looking as if it were contemplating some solar mystery, it had that same depth of amazement and bafflement, a kind of pure enchantment, void of cynicism or resentment.

"Where will you go?" he asked.

"I can't tell you."

"How long will you be?"

"I don't know. Two months maybe. But you have got to wait."

His eyes narrowed, having a last long look, then turning back to the fire, offended now.

"You're afraid to confide in your father," he said.

"It's better this way," I said.

"You must have to go very far, if it will take months."

"It might take less. I don't know."

"You've never been away from home before," he said, his inflection in semblance of a man disclosing some secret which was cleverly in his favor.

"I'm not going because I want a journey. I told you why I was going."

"You seem to be quite confident that your man will want to return with you."

"He'll come back."

"How did you learn his identity?"

"There's only one person who could have told me."

He snorted. "That's more than she ever told me."

"It might help her too, to see this man again." I watched him closely. If he knew his face did not show it. Perhaps he knew. I didn't know. Perhaps he knew but did not want to know, did not want to believe it, for as long as no one told him then it was not true. As I went up the stairs I turned for a moment to look at him again sitting before the fire, the old shawl wrapped about him, his face old and melancholy again, and I couldn't know what his eyes were seeing beyond the fire, beyond the hearth; but looking beyond the fire and beyond the hearth, beyond the house and the farm and Capstone.

3

I was up and ready before sunup. It seemed as if I hadn't slept at all, that my eyes were always opening upon the window waiting for the first of daylight to break the sky. Then I couldn't wait any longer and got up and dressed and went downstairs through the cold unlived living room and outside into the cold gray end of the night. I went to the stable and saddled Charl. I used one of Uncle Clay's old saddlebags and put the pistols into it. Then I led Charl out into the yard. The morning was going to be gray and quite chilly. The dew was moist upon my cheek.

Then Pa appeared on the porch and called me in. In the kitchen he made me drink some hot coffee and it wasn't until I began taking the coffee on my stomach that I realized how nervous or excited or maybe afraid I was; the coffee never seemed to hit anywhere but to fly about my stomach. Then Pa, hardly speaking at all, gave me a little bag of coins and an envelope with some paper money.

"You'll be on your own," he said, not looking at me, speaking slowly, sadly. "You'll come across people who'll want to help you. Some will be honorable Christians, some not. You'll have to choose between them."

Tom came down then, quiet and timid and impressed. Pa gave him warm milk and he never said a word, staring big-eyed at me while he drank it, following me out to the porch then with a white milk-mustache on his upper lip. He held Charl while I mounted. Sitting the horse I looked down into his face and it looked so small and afraid and anxious, the eyes so large and full under the short black bangs that lay flat on his forehead.

"You behave now," I said. He continued to gaze up with awe and wonderment. I leaned down and pushed at his hair and this—this humanizing gesture from what he had evidently been regarding not as his brother but some wonderous equestrian personage—relaxed him. He smiled and began backing away. I looked at Pa on the porch, he was standing on the top step, motionless, somber, gazing, probably still disapproving but caught helplessly in the great tide and surge and upheaval which he saw across the land, and he raised his hand to wave just as I turned Charl around and I didn't have the chance to wave right back and did not turn around again as I cantered across the yard under the massive unleaved branches of the maple, leaving it behind in its massive, rooted rage and went down the hard dustless morning stillness of the road.

It was about a half-hour after I'd been on the road that I heard the sound of a horseman behind me. I turned in the saddle and saw someone galloping down. I recognized the horse first: it was Mark, Rachel's mare; then I recognized the rider—Pete Mariah, crouched forward over Mark's shoulders, his forage cap pulled down. I waited. He began to slow, but he wasn't so skillful a rider and his horse reared on its hind legs as Pete reined it in and Pete looked for a moment like some wild general cheering on an attack. Then he was sitting before me, grinning, pushing the cap back over his untamable brown hair.

"What are you doing?" I asked.

"I heard," he said. "I was just around to the farm. Tom told me. I reckoned I'd better go along and see that you keep your feet dry."

"Do you know where I'm going?"

"Nope."

"Virginia."

"Good enough."

"You're just going to ride off like this?"

"Sure. You've got blankets there, haven't you?"

"Just one."

"That's good enough. We'll share it."

"How about your people?"

"Tom's going to tell 'em. They won't miss me. Say, we're not going to join up, are we?"

"No," I said.

"All right then, let's ride."

There was no point trying to dissuade him. So we began riding together, going slowly down the road.

"Where did you get Mark?" I asked.

"Your Pa."

"Does he know you're taking it to Virginia?"

"Well, he'll have it worked out by tonight."

"He'll call you a horse thief when we get back."

He took out his corncob and stuck it between his teeth. "I've been called that too," he said. "Now, Deacon, tell me why we're going to Virginia."

Daylight was beginning to crack the overcast in the east and here and there morning blue was beginning to show. The road was quiet. We passed a few men on their way down to the creek to work, passing them by in a gallop, beginning to move faster now.

The only reason Pete didn't guffaw and slap his thigh and say, "That Clay!" after I had told him, was because this time it was my sister.

PART TWO

CHAPTER 6

Pete stopped up ahead in the road and dismounted and kneeled down and picked something up and sniffed at it. When I rode up he showed me an empty canteen, holding it upside down.

"See this?" he said.

"What of it?" I said, sitting back in the saddle. He had been doing things like this ever since we had left Capstone several weeks ago—things like scrutinizing any strangers we came across on the road, interrogating children or old men or anyone else incapable of telling him to go to hell, eavesdropping in the taverns and stores where we stopped, following any tracks we happened to come across even if they led us into a marsh or swamp or (as they once did) upon an old man answering nature's call behind two large rocks in a pine wood; hoping to capture spies or stumble upon some priceless bit of intelligence that would crumble the defenses of Richmond or spring a bridge across the Rappahannock: doing this all during our long trip down the Jersey flatlands and down into Pennsylvania and now in Maryland as we approached the Potomac.

He rattled the canteen.

"It's just a canteen," I said. "There must've been plenty of soldiers. . . ."

"Is that so?" he said belligerently. He rubbed some dust from the canteen. Then I saw what he had seen first: the letters on the side of it—CSA. "See that?" he said ominously. He looked about, a feline wariness in his face, glancing about at the birch forest that stood close upon the narrow back road we were taking through the woods, the bleak leafless trees staring back, mournful in the chill late autumn air.

"They might've been here at one time or another," I said.

He wagged his finger. "Not lately. The fellow in the tavern in that last crossroads said they haven't been here for almost a year now. And this, "he said lifting the canteen with a gesture worthy of the footlights, "hasn't been here for more than a day, because you can still smell water in it."

"You think maybe we've blundered behind Rebel lines somehow?" I asked, half-jokingly, half not jokingly.

Pete's pained look made me ashamed of my ignorance. Then, patiently, he explained.

"It's probably from an infiltration, a patrol, spies. That damned Stuart and his cavalry come sneaking in everywhere. They might be somewhere just the other side of this timber."

"Well," I said, "if you're right, then I suggest we get out of here."

"You've got the pistols, haven't you?" he asked. He had an indestructible and incorrigible self-confidence that would have astonished and weakened a division of fanatics. He believed that Southern soldiers would melt and cower under his gaze; and if he had one of Uncle Clay's pistols in his hand that he could walk into Richmond over a path of fainted soldiers. Of course this immortal resolution had not yet been confronted with even the hum of a challenge, but he did have enough natural headstrong impetuousness to create a lot of trouble.

"Now, Pete," I said, using the firm fatherly tone I'd been using with him whenever his imagination began to boil up his impetuosity, "get on your horse."

"You'd give up a chance to wear Jeb Stuart's hat?" he asked, incredulous.

"Mount."

"I wish Clay was here," he muttered, throwing the canteen away into the dead leaves. He swung back up into the saddle.

"It'll be dark soon," I told him, "and we've got to find a place to bed down." In the beginning he had had me sleeping under the stars, but the nights were getting increasingly chilly.

So we started again. And now he'd got me nervous and I found myself watching the woods and watching the road, expecting at any second to have gray uniforms come sweeping out at us.

We rode for another half-hour before finally clearing the woods. We came to a small cluster of buildings standing at a crossroads. From the distance, in the twilit end of day, they looked deserted, but as we came nearer a man emerged from the central building—it was an inn—and tossed a bucket of water into the road. When he saw us he went back into the inn, his face turned at us until he disappeared back through the door, holding the empty bucket.

"Somebody's around, anyway," Pete said.

But there didn't seem to be any signs of habitation in any of the other houses. We passed an abandoned cornfield which was sickly and overgrown, beyond it the charred ruins of a homestead, its brick chimney standing against the gray day's end timeless and spectral. Holes in the ground marked the places where a fence had stood before being dismantled for firewood by someone, probably bivouacking soldiers. Approaching the houses we could sense the barren lifeless interiors, these feelings being corroborated by the sight of smashed windows and high weeds and a general air of abandonment.

We dismounted in front of the building with the sign Weemsboro Inn, the place where we had seen the man with the water bucket. It was a double-story building of gray clapboard with a porch running the length of its front. The upstairs windows had white lace curtains over them. The porch, supporting an upper porch with gray pillars, was sat by several empty rockers. The gray pillars had been inartistically carven with penknives and were covered with initials. We tied our horses in front of the water trough and mounted the porch steps and entered the inn.

There were three people inside. Evidently the one with the water bucket had alerted the other two because there was an air of anticipative curiosity; and they wanted to have a good hard uninhibited look at us before saying anything; and they did, a long, tart, speculative contemplation of us as we walked into the place and stood in the middle of the floor under a candle-glowing chandelier: looking at us as if we were not right there looking back at them.

They were two men and a woman. One of them—the one we had seen throwing the water—was sitting with his feet tossed upon a table. He was a rather unsavory, unbathed looking person, his clothing filthy and wrinkled, hanging over him with a dark contempt. His face was thin and sallow, raggedly bearded, bits of dead leaves clinging to the scraggly black hairs; his hair hanging down nearly to his eyes. In his hands he held a large carving knife. The other man stood behind the bar, resting forward on his arms. He was a large man, with hulking shoulders that massed behind his hunched body. His face was clean-shaven, round and thick with a small mouth. While the first one watched us with a rather doleful unfriendliness, this one observed us more keenly, shrewdly. The woman was sitting at one of the tables. She was rather buxom, with a chubby, heavily rouged, friendly face, her gaze containing a suggestive half-smile; but a depth in her concentrating eyes where the smile did not quite reach.

The one behind the bar spoke, finally.

"Boys," he said genially.

"Sir," I said.

"What can we do for you?"

"We'd take it kindly if you could put us up for the night."

"Well, we haven't been having so many visitors lately," he said. "People have left these parts since the war, and not many others have had the courage to come through. We'd appreciate your patronage."

"We can pay," I said.

"That's mighty cheerful words."

"Y'all got paper money, or gold?" the one at the table asked.

My eyes shifted to him. He watched me back with dull, doleful, unfriendly eyes.

"T'ain't none of your business, Simon," the other said. "The boys said they could pay. Don't mind Simon, boys. And this here's Rena. She's the cook, and she looks after the rooms." The woman nodded as we looked at her. "And my name's Matthew," he said, completing the introductions.

"My name's Jeff," I said. "This here's Pete."

"Well," Matthew said, still leaning on the bar, "now we're all acquainted. We're all old friends."

"Where you boys from?" Rena asked.

"Capstone," I said.

"Never heard of that," Simon said. He began paring his fingernails with the carving knife.

"It's on Long Island," I said. We were still standing in the middle of the floor; no one had invited us to come on further or sit down or go to the bar for a whiskey. I had an odd, disquieting feeling about these people and I began thinking of Uncle Clay's pistols in the saddlebag, how I wished I had them on me now.

"I heard of Long Island," Matthew said from behind the bar. "Never been there though."

He continued to watch us, and Simon did too. Rena sat at the table, still with her peculiar half-smile that might have been either coquetry or deviltry. Pete was looking back at her. (He would do that, strange place and hostile people notwithstanding; his appetites did not end at the table.)

"That's New York, isn't it?" Matthew said. "That Long Island."

"That's right," I said.

"You boys be Yankees then," Rena said.

"We be from New York, Miss Rena," Pete said pleasantly.

Yankees didn't call other Yankees, Yankees. So they weren't Yankees. We were in that part of the country where a man's allegiances couldn't be predicted any longer, where you'd run up against abolitionists in one town and secessionists in the next. And a lot of them had no allegiances to either side, but were simply opportunists, taking advantage of the wartime confusion wherever they could. These people were often more dangerous than those who were sworn to believe in something, moved by omnivorous appetites and often with blood so bad they could put a vampire on the water wagon.

"Where you boys all heading for?" Simon asked.

"We're just traveling," I said.

"This is a peculiar part of the country to be 'just travelin' in," he said looking at us from over his shoetops.

"The boys are too young to be soldiers," Rena said.

"We ain't soldiers," Pete said.

"We're just travelers," I said. "Looking for a bed for the night."

"Well you've come to the right place," Matthew said. "In fact it's the only place for miles around. There ain't no people, no farms or houses or anything, for miles and miles around."

"You folks wouldn't happen to know if there was any Rebel soldiers seen around here lately?" Pete asked.

There was a quiet moment; telltale, I thought. Then Matthew—they had seemed to defer to him for a moment and I knew then that he dominated here, for all the servility of his white apron and his place behind the bar—Matthew said, "No, boys. There ain't been any Confederate soldiers around here for a long, long time."

I waited for Pete to tell about the canteen. I just waited for that. And then I would wait for something real bad to happen, because if there were Rebel soldiers around here where they surely weren't supposed to be, then these people, I believed, didn't want anybody knowing about it. But Pete didn't tell. He didn't say anything at all about the canteen. Not even when Matthew said,

"Why, boy? Have you seen any?"

"I ain't seen a soul," Pete said.

"What makes you ask that then, boy?" Matthew asked in a sly way.

"Nothin'," Pete said. "Those things just concern me, that's all. When I left home my Pa said to look out for the Rebel army."

Rena laughed. It was a vibrant, youthful laughter and made her heavy cheeks rise up and make her eyes into slits. Evidently the laughter was infectious. Simon began to laugh too, throwing back his head like a man getting shaved and chortling, but Matthew didn't laugh until he'd had another straight, hard, inquiring look at Pete, wondering, I knew, what Pete had seen; then he laughed too, in short, forced, humorless chuckles.

Then the laughter stopped and Simon said, "That's a good one."

"Do you have any other guests?" I asked.

"Just one, boys," Matthew said. "Major Enright."

"U. S. Cavalry," Simon said from the table, with mock reverence.

"The Major is asleep upstairs," Matthew said. "He's very, very tired."

"If we're to stay the night," I said, "I reckon I'd better see to the horses."

"Simon can do that," Matthew said.

"It's all right," I said. "My horse has got a lot of temperament."

"Stable's around to the rear," Matthew said.

If Pete had come out with me I might have got him to ride off. But he stayed inside, looking at the woman. I led the horses around to the rear. But I didn't take them into the stable, because it was empty. If Major Enright was of the cavalry then his horse had ought to have been there. But it wasn't. So I led Mark and Charl past the stable into a stand of timber behind it, taking them quite a ways into it and settled them there. I took one of Uncle Clay's pistols out of the saddlebag and tucked it inside my shirt.

When I came back Pete was sitting at the table with the woman.

"I ordered us a dinner," he said. The woman laughed out loud, I don't know why, and clamped her hand down on Pete's for a moment, then got up and went around behind the bar into the kitchen.

We ate a dinner of soup and potatoes and beans and bread —there was no meat—and washed it down with cider. Later we sat on the porch with Matthew and Simon and smoked our pipes.

"It's an out of the way place at best," Matthew said. "Ever so often some Yankee soldiers come through, but that's all. There be some telegraph wires a few miles the other side of the wood and they stay there to guard them. Our neighbors all pulled out after Sharpsburg and went North. We're kinda in the middle here. We ain't on either side. We just tip our hats to all and wish them good luck."

We could hear the crickets singing in the dark, their terse little syllables beating placidly from every direction and I felt as if they were talking about us.

"What do they think of the war where you boys come from?" Matthew asked.

"They don't think too much about it," I confessed, and it made me feel strange for a moment, as if I had said I didn't believe in God. "I mean they're all behind it, but they don't think so much about it. They talk about crops and weather and all."

"Southern folks are different," Matthew said. "They'll die for it."

"Union soldiers die too," I said.

"I'll bet half of them can't tell you why."

"My uncle's in the Army," I said. "He takes great chances. People in Capstone think he's a Copperhead, but he goes right on taking the abuse and the slanders and does his work—real secret work too." But that didn't clear me, Uncle Clay's glory. I felt ashamed. I hadn't ever hardly thought about the war aside from the fact of seeing myself leading a charge next to the colors and chasing Rebels and winning praise from the general. It made me ashamed, as if somehow my instincts were wrong, selfish, censurable.

"You boys picked strange country for your traveling," Matthew said. "You aiming to cross the Potomac?"

"We might," I said.

"The Army won't let you, you know."

"We'll get across, if we have to."

"What time do you boys want to be roused tomorrow?"

"Sunup," I said.

Rena appeared in the doorway. "The room is ready," she said.

"Where'd you put the boys, Rena?" Matthew asked.

"In four. Next to the Major."

"Now you don't do any hollerin' up there, boys," Matthew said. "The Major's trying to sleep off forty-eight hours in the saddle."

The moon was just beginning to come up when we went upstairs.

The room wasn't much. The floors were bare. There was a big double bed with a big brass bedstead and some chairs, and in one corner, next to the bureau, a pot-bellied stove that was not in working order. But at least it was dry and quiet and there was no wind.

I sat down in one of the chairs. Pete sprawled out on the creaking bed.

"You know something, Deacon?" he said. "That Rena gal likes me. I wouldn't be a bit surprised if she. . . ."

"None of that," I said. "I don't like these people. I don't like the smell of them."

"Because they didn't tell about the Reb soldiers? Well, maybe they don't know about them, and maybe they just don't want to tell. They've got a Union major sleeping here, haven't they?"

"So they say. But his horse isn't in the stable. Where's his horse—especially if he's a cavalry officer? I'll tell you what they did: they stole his horse and gave it to the Rebs. So I put our horses out in the woods. Let them try and find them."

Pete didn't say anything. But I couldn't tell whether he was considering my suspicions or thinking about the woman—a man's face looks the same about both things sometimes.

"You can go to sleep, but not me," I said. "I ain't even taking off my boots."

"What've you got there?" he asked.

"Uncle Clay's pistol. I'm keeping it handy."

"Well, they might want to rob us sure enough. That dirty-looking one was sure interested in our money."

I looked out the window. The moon was rising higher, shedding a thin, cold light over the treetops. The room became chilly. I couldn't hear anything from downstairs or from any of the other rooms. I wondered what they were doing, our three hosts. Pete's eyes were closed.

"You going to sleep?" I asked.

"Yep," he said.

"Well, not me," I said, pushing the pistol down into my belt.

I really meant to stay awake too. Even as my eyes were shutting and I felt my head nodding over my chest and my fingers letting go their grip on Uncle Clay's pistol, I kept telling myself with a striving of consciousness that I was merely closing my eyes for this moment, feeling the deep luxuriant darkness draping over me like a shroud.

I don't know how long it was for: perhaps a minute, perhaps more, because then the sound was waking me, opening my eyes and jerking up my head, making my fingers go off in a trembling search for the handle of the pistol. It wasn't much of a sound, abrupt, surreptitious—over before it had hardly begun; but it was a complete and total sound, not like something done by the wind or inherent in the house's oldness, not vague or passing, stopped and suspended in the chilly dark and like an eye or something alive and breathing there (not the perpetration but the sound itself); like a tongue that has clucked: not much of a sound but enough to unbalance the uneasy equipoise of my sleep. I sat erect, immediately, clearly, tensely awake; it was as if I had never been asleep at all. The sound had come from the door, and now, soundlessly, the door was moving, like something afloat in the dark, then stopping; and someone was standing there, revealed to the moon-tipped dark but not yet to me, someone breathing little currents of palpable stillness, poised and tense as though on the threshold of a mighty stride.

I was going to wait. But I couldn't.

"Who's there?" I asked, my voice quiet—too quiet, I felt; not strong and assertive as it should have been.

Rena came through the doorway. She closed the door behind her and the sound came again as it clicked shut. She came through the dark at me.

"What do you want?" I asked.

"Shhh," she said.

I could smell the perfume. It was a sweet, outdoors smell, but not quite outdoors, too subtle, as if straining to be, or do, something that it wasn't, couldn't be; rising off her flesh and effusing a subtle odor that was almost bewitching but which failed. But yet I had never inhaled it before and took two deep breaths of it and by that time she was before me, her face leaned near, one hand on my shoulder. And then the perfume was like a cloud in my face, like an anesthetic, and her warm, heavy lips were clinging to mine. I just sat, my eyes wide and startled staring against her cheeks, my breathing drowned in the perfume.

Then her face went away and I was still sitting startled and wordless and gazing.

"You don't know how long it's been since a young man has come into this place," she whispered, her voice low and heavy with a tense breathing. She was waiting. Then she stopped waiting. I pushed her hand away from me.

"Come into the next room with me," she said.

"Go away," I said.

"We can have a beautiful night," she murmured.

"No," I said.

"Please," she whispered, still bent toward me, the moon glinting across her eyes for a moment.

"No," I said, not whispering. It woke Pete. The bed creaked as he turned over and sat up on one elbow, looking at us.

"What's that?" he said. He rubbed his eyes, either to rub away the sleep or to make certain he was not seeing an illusion. Rena stood up straight, her dress rustling.

"Go back to sleep," I said to him. Then to Rena: "You've roused him."

"Miss Rena," Pete said, as though he were seeing a saint.

She went to him. He was amazed. He ran his hand through his touseled hair.

"Your friend doesn't like me," she said to him, her voice low, hurt, like she was talking through a pouting mouth.

"He don't understand women," Pete said.

She sat down next to him and put her face close to his and I turned away, not shy or embarrassed, not anything like that, but angry and upset because I knew this wasn't right, that we were guests here—guests of unfriendly hosts to begin with, and here was their woman in our room in the middle of the night. Then Pete was leaning over me talking a hot streak into my ear.

"This is no ordinary woman, Jeff . . . plump and warm as a summer melon . . . no harm done if . . . you go off to another room so's we don't have to warm up another bed . . . fifteen minutes . . . nobody has to know . . . we can't very well insult the lady of the house. . . ."

The lady? The lady! I was going to tell him. . . . But it was no good to argue with him, I knew. Especially in that kind of situation. The sooner it was done the better, I felt. So I left them alone and went out into the hall, my hand resting on the butt of the pistol which was stuck in my belt. I stood out there in the dark for a few minutes, then I heard them giggle in there and I edged away from the door, self-conscious.

I found myself standing in front of the next room, where they said the Union major was asleep. I put my ear against the door and stood like that for a minute maybe, but heard nothing. So I tapped lightly with my fingertips, wanting to wake him and not wanting to. Getting no response, I put my hand on the doorknob and quietly began turning it until the door was moving out ahead of me and I was walking into the dark, chilly room. Through the still, moon-watered dark I could see the outline of someone lying on the bed. Coming closer, I could see, as it lay under the moon's faint fall, the man's face in deep unfathomable repose. He had a short, carefully kept beard that lay just above the top button of his jacket. He was lying upon the covers, in full uniform, the moon glistening like a melancholy eye on his scabbard. It was strange, I thought, to be asleep this way. I whispered his name, stepping closer. I watched the closed eyes, waiting for them to flicker. I stood over him then. I reached down and touched his shoulder, then pushed his shoulder. I suppose then something inside of me was wiser and more alert and more certain than my thoughts which that moment dwelled like an old woman's upon how peaceful and deep-fallen his sleep was; for this other thing, this realistic and relentless thing, made my other hand pull up the pistol. I saw then, through the gradually melting dark, the mark that came up from under the beard and went under his ear and I pushed aside the bristly beard and saw the dark savage rip that looped his throat from ear to ear and then his head rolled away from me and my fingers felt the crusts of congealed blood.

I whirled away then and rushed toward the door, flinging it aside. I ran out into the hall just as the yell came from the next room, from Pete's panting lungs. Simon was just coming out of the room and I stopped, leveling the gun.

"Hup, Matty!" he cried.

"Pete!" I yelled.

Simon came at me, the carving knife in his hand, but he stopped when he saw the pistol. Then I heard something crash in the room, something hit the floor and tumble across it and Pete yell again.

"Back up!" I yelled at Simon. "Throw off the knife!" He threw the knife over the railing and a moment later it clashed on the floor below. Then I went on, stopping in the doorway. I turned my head for a moment and saw them roughing it on the floor, Pete fighting like some maddened ghost in his long, white drawers, Rena frozen in her running toward me, her long, yellow hair floating over naked shoulders.

"Simon!" she shrieked. He was coming at me—in that split second of head-turning I had lost him. I turned and fired; fired, actually, before I turned, the pistol roaring with a white flash, the bullet flying wildly; but it was enough to stop Simon, enough to terrify him and send him into mad flight. He ran like an animal, like some deformed thing, in a half-crouch, his shoulders hunched up over his head. He ran until he struck the wall and then descended in a wild clattering that sounded like six men.

I ran into the room then, past Rena who glared at me, and with the pistol's butt cracked Matthew on the head. His head came up with a jolt as if he had just thought of something, and then, from his kneeling position from which he had begun to choke the life from Pete, he fell over unconscious.

Then we were running, out of the room and down the stairs. All the time Pete was chattering something about it having been a plan to separate us and why I didn't stop and shoot Rena who had deceived him in the crucial matter of love.

Then we were on the porch, in the night, taking the steps in a single leap, our feet hitting the ground simultaneously with abrupt impact and Pete was following me around the back of the house toward the woods where I had left our horses. We didn't stop running until we had reached the horses and it felt as if we had left behind us a noisy storming forest of sounds and grasping fingers.

We mounted the astonished beasts and began plunging through the woods, Charl and Mark crashing through branch and brush with incredible ferocity and devotion. We didn't stop until we came to a clearing, and only then for a moment. Then I looked at him, and Pete had a look at himself too for the first time. He was sitting atop Mark still in his long white underwear. He appeared astonished, as if his shirt and trousers had just this instant flown from him.

"Goddamn!" he cried.

"They butchered that major," I said. "I saw him, his throat cut from here to. . . ."

"Never mind him. I've got no trousers," Pete said.

"You don't deserve any," I said. "You pulled one hell of a fine stunt back there. They could've murdered us both."

"How could I know? No woman ever did that before."

"I thought you knew all about women," I said. "You once said you could write a book about women."

"I said should, not could," he said sourly. "I'm wiped out," he said. "I've lost all my worldly belongings."

"Your pipe, your tobacco and your penknife," I said. "And almost your life along with them."

"I could've taken that fellow," he said stubbornly.

"He had his hands around your throat."

"I was going to play dead."

"For a long time, in another second."

"He came right into the room," Pete said. "I thought it was you. I said 'Wait a minute,' and then he jumped me. I couldn't fight back, never had a chance."

"Because you were in heat."

"Partly."

We began riding again. We didn't breathe peaceful until we struck a road.

"If it wasn't for Uncle Clay's pistol," I said, "we'd be lying there alongside that major. That fellow Simon had the knife all wetted up."

"Did you kill him?" Pete asked.

"No. I didn't even aim. I just fired without looking."

"We ought to go back and take care of them. I'd like to fix them up good."

"A better idea would be to send you back to Capstone right now, just the way you are, so everybody can see what a damn fool you are."

"I never thought it was going to be what it was," he said, contrite, and hurt. "She told me she loved me."

"Did she tell you you were the first young man she'd seen in months?"

"How did you know?"

"She loved us both," I said, kicking Charl's flanks, making Pete ride hard to keep up.

CHAPTER 7

We spent the rest of the night in the saddle. When daylight began to filter smokily through the trees Pete became afraid to ride any further the way he was, afraid we might just encounter some fluffy young lady riding under a parasol. It didn't bother me though; I was hoping he might learn a lesson from all this, although my confidence in this was dim, for what would be a mere lesson to him would have to be a catastrophe by other standards. But besides his embarrassment he was beginning to rattle with shivering, so we dismounted and made a fire and cooked breakfast. Pete put the blanket around himself and sat as close to the fire as he could. Some hot coffee helped lift his temperature a trifle. Then we chewed some hardtack that we'd got from some soldiers a few days before. The hardtack was like pieces of concrete and I remembered now with more appreciative understanding somebody saying that if we made our soldiers eat enough of it before going into battle it would make their bellies impregnable to Rebel shot.

We'd bought a map from a fellow in New Jersey. The truth was we'd got lost right there in New Jersey the second day out. We found it wasn't just enough to ask people which way was "South." Not everyone knew—and it was these people, kindly and well-meant though they were, who seemed to supply us with directions. At one point the only thing that interrupted our journey "South" was the Atlantic Ocean, a fine body of water, but unfortunately (or maybe fortunately) it pitched off in an easterly direction. But you had to know more than merely which way lay South, you had to know roads and fords and towns. So we bought a map from a fellow who ran a feed and grain establishment and who guaranteed the map's accuracy. (And an accurate, up-to-date map was a scarce item, it seemed. He said that even the Army sometimes had a devil of a time finding out where it was going and how.) We saw Baker Station written on it, just the other side of a dark line that curved and trembled around Virginia called the Potomac River, about three hand spans down from the place in New Jersey where we bought the map. It didn't seem far at all, nor too complicated.

The map brought us along pretty good. Occasionally one of the roads it showed led us into a swamp or an unpassable forest, but we were never too far off. When we did run across real difficulty we sought out the local parsonage and obtained our directions there. Pete said that if a man could help to get somebody's soul all the way to heaven then he ought to know how to direct two God-fearing youths to a place as handy as Baker Station. And, too, it never hurt our stomachs or our haversacks either for talking to these men.

When we began passing through towns that we saw written

on the map just where they were supposed to be, then we began to trust it and believe in it.

I took it out now and opened it up and had a long hard look at it. I reckon I knew it by heart by this time—I even dreamed about it a few times.

"We must be getting close to Baker Station," I said.

"Never mind Baker Station," Pete said. "I've got to get me some duds."

"Maybe we'll come to a town soon," I said. I put the map down and looked at him. "As I recall," I said, "your grandpa used to walk around all day in his underwear and it never seemed to bother him. I reckon you're just not the man your grandpa was."

"He was missing a couple of bricks to begin with," Pete said sourly. "You couldn't get him to wear duds nohow."

"What'd he do in the cold months?"

"Why do you ask? You're not interested anyway."

"Sure I am."

"He'd put more underwear on over the other underwear."

"I reckon he'd have understanding for you now."

"I tell you, Deacon, I'll catch mortal cold this way."

He'd lost the cap Uncle Clay had given him, too, and this probably upset him as much as the loss of the trousers.

"He'll get you another one," I said.

"How soon you think we'll catch up to him?"

"Soon enough." I folded up the map and put it back inside my shirt.

"What do you think he'll say to you?"

This was the first time since we had left Capstone that either of us had alluded to Uncle Clay. As I sat before the fire watching the gray smoke lift off into the morning air

I realized that I had been intentionally avoiding thinking of Uncle Clay—I don't know why. Maybe I was afraid to see him. It would be asking a considerable lot to ask him to leave his work and come back with us. But then when I told him of Rachel's way, and of Pa on the brink of committing a murder, then I could see him whirling his horse and rushing back with us to Capstone.

"I reckon he'll see only one thing to say," I said.

"Suppose he can't get away?"

"He'll get away," I said tersely, feeling a quick resentment. "Uncle Clay can do whatever he wants."

"I reckon we'll be dancing to a wedding then," Pete said.

"Maybe."

"If he hurries."

"That's not so funny," I said. I threw some hot coffee over the fire onto his feet. It made him jump.

"Damn it, Deacon," he said, rubbing his feet.

The sun was coming through the trees now, swirling a deft translucence through the woods. Gradually things were beginning to appear, the leaves with their bright death-stains, and the trees and the rocks, all there, there again, reappearing as stolid and patient as it had disappeared the night before and a thousand nights before; a kind of sullen inevitability about it, as if in its gnarled and mossy trunks and up and out to its utmost tapered twig it could already sense the blow and ring of the inevitable ax. Morning came like an assuaging, settling tranquilly upon the somber old wood which in its turn grudgingly absorbed its renewal and continued.

I began putting out the fire. Pete did his share by expectorating through his teeth.

"What about my trousers?" he asked.

"I reckon Simon's wearing them now. His were about shot."

"A man can't go on riding about in his long johns—especially in a strange country."

"And with a war on, too."

"That's right."

"I reckon Pa would say you're being properly punished," I said.

"Even your Pa, who hates me, would take more pity on me than you do."

"And even my Pa, who never laughs, would become ten years younger from laughing if he could see you."

For awhile Pete rode with the blanket around him, like an Indian. But then the sun started to get warm and he had to take it off. We rode for maybe another half-hour when all of a sudden a shot rang out and we heard something whizz over our heads like a wild bird, fluttering the leaves, the echo booming off into the woods. Mark was startled by it (he'd always belonged to Rachel and was accustomed to a more gentle way of life) and he took off before Pete could do anything to stop him and off they went down the road, Mark—probably sore enough from all the previous, unaccustomed abuse he'd been subjected to—tearing away with Pete bouncing all over the saddle in his long johns trying to hold on. I was about to take off after him when I heard voices yell at me to stay put.

Three soldiers came out from behind a stone wall. One of them was holding a smoking rifle, pointing it in my general direction. Their blue uniforms were covered with dust and grass stains. They were a rather seedy-looking lot, weary and laconic and cynical. Their jaws were going round and round with sullen independence, each ejecting brownish tobacco streams in streaks over the road from time to time. They were looking up at me, their faces set with suspicion.

"Get off that horse, boy," one said, gesturing with his rifle.

"For who?" I asked.

"For me," he said. "For the U. S. Government."

"Why'd you fellows shoot at us?" I asked.

The one with the rifle—I could see now his yellow sergeant's marking on his blue sleeve—said: "We didn't shoot *at* you, we shot toward you. There's a difference."

"A difference," another said, talking morosely through a long, thick beard that was a genuine fire hazard, "between dead and alive." He turned his head aside and shot a prodigious streak of tobacco juice clear across the road.

So I dismounted. The sergeant lowered his rifle.

"Where you from?" he asked.

"New York."

"What are you doing around here?"

"Just traveling."

"Who's your friend?"

"He's from New York too."

"He was wearing a mighty peculiar uniform."

"Wasn't no uniform," I said. "That was his long johns. He lost his clothes in a place last night."

"His horse'll run out soon," the sergeant said. "We'll find him later. Now you'd better step along with us."

I soon found out what it was all about. These three were part of a detail that was guarding the telegraph wires in that area. And it seemed they had had good reason for firing "toward" us, for a number of Rebel cavalrymen were reported to be roving in the area, some of whom in fact had already succeeded in cutting some of the wires. I told about having found the canteen and this helped to confirm what they already knew. I told, too, about Major Enright and our experience the night before (or most of it, anyway), and the officer in charge of the camp—for the three soldiers brought me there—Captain Morris, dispatched ten men to go to Weemsboro to arrest the three assassins and recover the major's body.

I was able to convince the Captain that I was from New York and that my heart was pure of malevolence. He even apologized for the shot that had been fired "toward" me, and went on to say that if I were indeed a loyal Union supporter then I should be glad to have found our soldiers so diligent in the performance of their duty.

They had a small camp in a clearing marked by fresh-axed tree stumps. Nearby was a forest of dead dogwood, many of which had been cut down by the soldiers for use as fuel and for other purposes. I left Charl in the little corral they had built and wandered around the camp and stared at things. Three long rows of wedge tents created two level and unlittered avenues one of which was called Broadway by a plank nailed to a tree. Most of the soldiers were indifferent to me. It was the first time I'd ever seen that many soldiers at once and I gaped at them. I guess I was a trifle disappointed. Many of them were busy with what seemed to be highly unsoldierly business—washing their clothes or polishing their boots or mending their garments with exasperating and unskilled fingers; looking rather tame and innocuous, even with the pyramid of stacked rifles in the center of each avenue.

A stocky, thick-muscled soldier was sitting in front of one of the A-shaped tents. He was sitting on a small inverted barrel, one hand emerging upward from crossed arms to hold his pipe in his mouth. From this fixed and steady attitude he was contemplating me, his eyes moving reflectively with me as I crossed before his field of vision. Then he seemed to have made his mind up about something and he called to me. I stopped.

"C'mere," he said. He let go of the pipe and unfolded his arms and rested his hands on his knees.

I came up to him. His eyes fixed somberly and suspiciously upon my face.

"Yes sir?" I asked.

He did not immediately reply, but continued to watch me, sitting there before the open tent in ponderous immobility, meditating some deep problem. Then he became very still; not that he had been moving before, but now he became an absolute study in stillness, as if not just his breathing but even his blood-flow and heart-tick had suspended. Then he asked me.

"You know how to write?"

"Yes sir," I said.

He watched me gravely. His breathing was on again. Now a slight, barely perceptible wrinkle came into the corners of his eyes, and this tiny sign exuded and confessed the shyness and perhaps mortification which he had striven to overcome.

"I need a letter writ for me," he said.

"Do you have pen and paper?" I asked.

"Yes," he said. He moved then, got up and went into the tent, bending his forage-capped head and yellow-suspendered back and emerging the same way a moment later, holding a sheet of slack yellow paper and a small pen. He looked around at the other tents, then to me, and said,

"Inside would be better."

I followed him into the tent. It was not very commodious inside, with about six or seven square feet of floor space, most of it covered with straw. Several bedrolls were tucked in one corner. A small stove stood in the center under the horizontal pole, its rusty pipe passing up through a hole in the apex. There were several wooden boxes standing about and I sat down on one and drew another against my knees to employ as a desk. The soldier sat on another and faced toward the outside, staring off at the trees and the sky over them. A tiny inkstand stood on another box and I dipped the pen into it and lifted it out and poised it over the page.

"You ready?" he asked.

"Yes," I said.

He folded his arms. Then he crossed his legs. I watched his face, waiting. It was melancholy, contemplative, but a detachedness akin to simple vision soon softened it as he sought, apparently, to transport himself from here away to some aloof, insular place where it would be easier for him.

"To my dear wife," he began, his voice a trifle formal, self-conscious, and slow, and not for my benefit I felt, but because he wanted to dwell on what he was saying and what it was making him see. "I am well and hope you and the babies are enjoying a like blessing. I think often of you and the little ones. When you next write please put the pen in their hands and let them mark the page even though they cannot write, so I can see something of them." He paused for near a minute, his eyes musing on the far-off. Then he resumed, again slow, intimate. "I was to ask the Captain about a furlough this morning, but we are shy of men just at this moment and it would not be fair to leave just now, even if I would be granted the time. I miss you and the little ones, only God knows how much, and the farm and home; but you know we're doing the right thing here. At night we sit before the fires and the men speak of their homes and their loved ones and each tells how much he misses them all, but each man of us is united in the opinion that we must be here and remain until the job is done. Please send a sweater, as soon the weather will start in turning chilly. I am thinking of the time when the Lord will unite us as one again. Your loving husband, Burt."

He stopped. It seemed he was letting the warm home-images flow from his mind, letting them fade off before his eyes. Then he looked at me.

"Have you got that?" he asked.

"Yes," I said.

"I don't write so well," he said. He took the letter and looked at it, just looked, not read, because he evidently could not read so well either. He nodded. He folded the letter and put it into his breast pocket. "Well," he said, "you know my name but I don't know yours."

"Jeff Taylor," I said.

"I'm obliged for your favor."

"Where will the letter go?" I asked.

"Home, to Elmira."

"You've got a farm there?"

"Yes."

"How old are the babies?"

"Two and three. Two little girls." He appeared pleased to have been asked, smiling sadly through his beard. "I miss them awful bad." Then, as if regretting that he had shown this moment of sentiment, he stood up, his attitude changed, proud, aloof. With his palm feeling the letter in his pocket, he left the tent and walked off.

I got up and left the tent too, moving idly through the camp, staring at the soldiers. Some were carrying armloads of wood and dumping them into a little wooden shed. Two others were off at a far corner digging slowly and without enthusiasm—latrines, I suspected. Still others were lounging about, doing nothing. Passing one of these latter I heard myself hailed.

"See here, boy," the soldier said sitting up from the prone position in which he had been relaxing on the grass, "what are you doing here anyway?"

"Just traveling," I said.

"Lookin' for the war, eh?" he asked. "Well, it's close enough if you don't watch out."

"Have you been in the fighting?" I asked naïvely.

"I've a scar to show for it," he said. He removed his cap and showed me a rather fresh-looking red furrow along the side of his head, running his finger down it. "See her?" he said. He put the cap back on and pulled the visor down toward the bridge of his nose, a flicker of pride in his plain, clean-shaven face. "Got that a whiles back. You can see by that the small difference between life and death, eh?"

"Where did you get it?"

"In the woods hereabouts. We got ourselves a reb major, though. Got him good. Say, what about a good game of checkers?"

"I don't play," I said.

"Don't, eh?" I don't think he believed me, but he let it pass. "Well, if there's one thing I miss back home it's the game of checkers those boys used to play." He chuckled and shook his head. "I miss that, yessir."

"Where is your home?" I asked, sitting down on the wooden box in front of the tent.

"New York State. Way up 'bove Lake George. Yes, I miss that old place," he said wistfully. "Fall's the best time of year up there too. You never saw such colors as you see in the mountains at just this time."

Just then several soldiers on horseback went riding through the camp, fast and loud, and disappeared up the road. The soldier stood up and watched after them, hooking his thumb inside his suspender. Then he sat down again, crossing his legs under him.

"There they go," he said. "Gonter play cat-and-mouse in that damned wood again with those rebs. Gawd, how them graybacks can become part of the foliage. They'll be standing there close enough to twist your button and you never see them and the next thing you know is you're poorer'n skim piss."

"Is that what happened to you?" I asked.

"Yes, sonny. The grayback came right out at me and fired

at me from here to there," he said holding his hands apart to show. "Knock me right down on my hams, but I gave it to him good. My ball went clean through him."

"You killed him?" I asked.

A note of horror must have thinned my voice because he showed me a long, compassionate look, then nodded.

"That's the game we're playing here," he said. "We've had to bury some of our own too. Oh yes, the rebs are hellbent to cut those wires, but we're just as dead set against them doing it." He chuckled. "Who'd a-ever thought I'd be caring about some telegraph wires strung through a place in Maryland I never ever heard of." Then he frowned, staring down at his hands. "Sometimes I ask myself why I volunteered to come down here. Didn't have to you know. Left a real burden on the family too." He reflected pensively for a moment. Then he seemed to remember something, or perhaps define it. "I was standing in the field with my hand on the plow and I looked up at the mountains way off and I found myself thinking, 'I got to go off to the war.' Just like that. Just like the mountains themselves had a-told it to me. So I went, right from that moment. Left a real burden on the family. But I told them what good would our home and family life be if we have no country to enjoy it in? If the country perishes then we'll all be better off if we perish with it. There," he said, privately pleased, as if he had finally solved some puzzling riddle of long standing. "That's why."

There. He had explained his reason, his purpose. Given me an answer to something I had not even asked. I sought to understand, but I couldn't quite do it. Why would the country perish? After all, this was not a war like the European wars I'd read about in school. The vanquished would not have his country overrun and his institutions toppled and his statesmen shot and his borders effaced. Why would Capstone perish if the North lost the war? No Southerners would come up and take our farm or drive Judge Stetterson from his office or put a troop of soldiers in front of the Dooley House. Our trees would not split nor our streams dry nor our vines wither. Would our meadows turn to dust or our cows give sour milk or our roads turn to water?

But yet there was something happening, there had to be; something vast and mysterious; something tremendous enough to send soldiers back broken and bent and blind and still inspire others to go eager and fearless to take their places. Soldiers like this man with the scar who longed for his checker game and whose leaving—voluntary leaving—had left a burden upon his family. Like the men who had ridden off into the woods to chase Rebels who could stand five feet away with a rifle and not be seen. Men did not thus gamble their lives so lightly.

The Captain invited me to share some food with him and we sat outside around a fire and went through a meal of cornbread and coffee and salt pork. After the meal the two other officers who had eaten with us rode out to their posts and I remained at the fire with Captain Morris. He was a serious, studious-looking man with a neat lay of black hair which he combed carefully to one side. His interest in why I was there persisted.

"It's no place to be wandering about," he said.

"We're careful," I said.

"You rode right through a wood where we know the Rebels are. If they'd of seen you you would be buried in there now."

"I guess we were lucky," I said, giving Pete some thought, wondering how far Mark had carried him. The Captain had sent a man on out to look for him. I lighted my pipe and rested back against a tree. The Captain continued to stare at me, his face curious, still a trifle mistrustful, earnest, a rather sensitive and intelligent face.

"What part of New York are you from?" he asked.

"Capstone," I said. "My Pa has a farm there."

"Are you down here looking for someone?"

"Sort of," I said, unable to tell him a full lie.

"A soldier?"

"No."

"It must be pretty important business to have brought you so far, and at such a risk."

"Yes, sir, I would say it's pretty important business."

"You realize, of course, that you're going to have to go back."

I didn't say anything to that. I wasn't going to go back, but there was no sense in telling him that.

"This is a very dangerous place just now," he said.

"You're here," I said.

"We're soldiers," he said quietly, earnestly, and with a quiet dignity. "We're here for a reason." And the way he said it, the way he looked at me made me feel that his reason was far greater than it sounded, than mere words could make it. His reason was more than looking for wire-cutting Rebel cavalrymen.

"It seems," he went on, "that at the moment only the soldiers understand the reason." His voice carried more regret than resentment. "There is no glory down here. It's hard times. There's nothing but death and pain and fear, and then hunger and fatigue and lice and filth and sleeping in the mud and the rain; and no time for sorrows or regrets. But we have our purpose in being here, and for that purpose we are willing to endure." He was saying it for my benefit. He could see—to my shame and embarrassment—that my mind was innocent of the higher purposes. But it was not a lecture; he was saying it in a simple, direct, quite conversational way. "The importance of being here, for many of us, is underlined by the fact that we don't have to be here. We're volunteers."

"You volunteered?" I asked.

He nodded. "We're all part of a volunteer regiment. We all came willingly—not anxiously, mind you, not for glory or swords or battle flags, but with a willingness to show that we believe in our purpose, that we will die for it. You'll find every class of man among us—farmer and clerk and laborer and professional man. I was a school teacher myself before the war; I hope to be a school teacher again when it's over."

I pulled thoughtfully on my pipe. The Captain's eyes seemed very sad. At first I thought they were tired, but then I could see that it was a great, soulful sadness.

"A lot of them from our town joined up," I said.

"I know," he said. "And I'm sure that most of them can't put into words the reason why, but they feel it. They know just why they're here fighting and dying. After it's over they'll go back home and most of them will forget why they fought, and that's probably a good thing too; let their minds be concerned with more peaceful pursuits."

"Where is your home?" I asked.

"A little town just outside of Albany."

"This is the first time I've ever been away from home," I said.

"It's not a good thing to be away from home."

It made me feel very odd. And it made me think of the men from Capstone who had gone off to fight. I had never thought before of them being lonesome for their homes, of sitting somewhere in a trench or a hut or marching through a strange town seeing other people's homes and thinking of Capstone where I was walking or working or riding, and it seemed to me that something had been passing over my head the whole time while I went on ignorant of it; but Pa had known of it, was always talking of it and now I began to feel it for the first time, began to feel the power of the passion and compassion and the absolute woe that he would feel whenever he talked of the war. And it made me feel less a man than ever before, and made me wonder if the time would ever come when I would be a man in all the respects that Captain Morris was, if that perhaps immaturity was too poor an excuse for too many things.

"Your pipe has gone out," the Captain said.

"It wants attention," I said.

"So you see that this is not a playground down here," he said. "Many young fellows often mistake it for that. But they soon learn differently. Would you like more coffee?"

I heard him say it but I didn't answer. I guess I was trying to conjure something profound, to fill the void, to create some profound and momentous thought that would elevate me sufficiently to understand the higher purpose that the Captain and the men around me and Pa too understood.

"It's not an easy thing to explain," the Captain said. "You can only put part of it into words. The rest of it you have to find out for yourself, when you see men hurling themselves against a blazing breastworks, into certain death; see them walking through smoke and canister. You say to yourself, 'For what?' The mind isn't immediately prepared to answer. But then, if you want to know badly enough, you begin to feel it, sense it, and you know then that there is something greater than man and that he knows it and is struggling to achieve that greatness, reaching forever upward in an effort to extend his soul. Each man carries it inside of himself, the same as he carries his own food and water and reads his own Bible and meditates the words in his own way. Most of them can't find phrases for their ideals, and maybe it's better that way, because it becomes more personal and more sacred and more urgent.

"We're fighting to save our country, Jeff. Now, some countries are old, a hard war such as this is would destroy them. Other countries just crumble from old age, from the erosion of their own decay. History is full of them. But our country is young. You fight to save something that is young. It would be simple enough to say, 'Go your way, Southern brother.' And maybe we in our lifetime would not even know that they are gone. But the decay would set in. We would be two parts dying rather than one thriving. Eventually both would die and our Revolution, our Constitution—all of it will have been for nothing. We would become a little collection of States, like in Europe, with petty alliances, perhaps even with monarchies, like in Europe, with endless, senseless warring and bickering. Ask yourself if this wasn't meant to be a single nation. Bounded on the north by ice, on the east and west by great oceans, on the south by water and by friendly peoples. What other nation has such geographic peace and strength?"

"We never think of it like that," I said.

"The same as we never think about our homes. We simply walk into them and close the door and sit down into the good life and never think about how fortunate we are. Well, our country is our greater home, and I'll wager you, Jeff, you've never taken thought to see how much you love it or how desperately you would fight to defend it."

"No," I said.

"That's because we let it go as love of God," he said. And, strangely, something inside him seemed to respond to that as sadly, wistfully, his eyes shifted and gazed out beyond the treetops. For a little while he reflected wistfully. When his voice resumed it seemed to be speaking to that vague, misty place in the sky. "We love God, yes, as we should and must, but we must love our country too, in a separate way, the way we have separate and special loves for our parents and our sweethearts. No single love can embrace them all. But love of country is often obscured, because there isn't always a complete understanding or an appreciation of what its existence means. Next to God it should be our greatest love and worship. And you can see how many good men have come to realize this, now that their country's existence has been challenged. They know what they're fighting for all right—a deep historical purpose."

I remembered that last: a historical purpose. I would remember it through the next few days and then forever, to the end of my life. And I thought: love of God, yes, and love of country too; and these men given the opportunity to manifest that love and doing it, burying with their own seared and broken bodies all hypocrisy and platitude, carrying the flags in their own fists for a historical purpose which few of them understood or could express but which they could feel in their hearts.

"This is going to be a long and costly and tragic war," the Captain said, looking at me again. "By the time it is over half our country, or maybe even all of it, will lay in desolation. Homes and farms and towns and even cities will lay in ashes. Human lives will be lost beyond computation. But it is necessary that this war be waged, that all losses in life and property be endured, for it is a war that is being fought in the name of democracy's survival." Self-consciously, he smiled. "Big, important-sounding words, eh, Jeff?" Then the smile slowly passed and it was as if his face had aged. "If we are successful then modern history will begin a new era; our ordeal will mark a turning point in the history of human freedom. But such an achievement cannot be won without pain, and we're undergoing that pain now, purging ourselves of our sins with fire and blood. The monster slavery is now in its death struggle. And we're suffering too for having permitted it to extend for so long. This is an ordeal for the entire nation, for every man, woman, and child. It's a moment in history. You're living it, young man, you're part of it. We all are.

"War is an ugly, dirty business. It is horrible. The most horrible thing in which mankind can involve itself. And the longer it goes on the worse it is for men, for it can change them. Men are being compelled to do things which they don't want to do, never dreamed of doing, things which come antagonistically to their natures; sudden, desperate things. It is all a sudden, bewildering call to valor. But they've been responding, and responding with all the greatness and nobility of which men are capable. But it is a dangerous thing. It can take the decent and the God-fearing and poison them. Men were not intended to be subjected to the brutal slaughter of their brethren. Men are not only maimed and wounded in war, but their moral values can be altered and impaired. They can come to a point where they lose all respect for human life and decency and righteousness. Because of its own barbaric nature war brings out the worst that there is in men, and the longer it goes on the longer these men go on being victims of themselves, and through no particular fault of their own beyond being human. I've seen men in my own company suddenly reveal the basest sides of their natures, men who had probably never even dreamed evil before they came to war. We send out foragers and instead of coming back with food they bring back silk dresses and silverware. A farmer fighting to save his money from being stolen is shot down in cold blood. This sort of thing goes on and becomes worse. War creates cynics and opportunists and sometimes even killers, and when it is over these men return home with these unapparent diseases and permeate society. So we must end it quickly, not merely for the sake of life and limb, but so that these men can forget as quickly as possible what they saw and did and endured.

"Each time a war is fought the mainstream of history is

polluted a little more. Certain advances are made, yes, but when these are weighed against the poisons that are released into the blood and the hatred that becomes fixed in the hearts, they are hardly worth it. War was our last resort. It isn't the only way to resolve issues, but all other ways have been exhausted. So now the conflict is on and we must win it as quickly as we can."

He leaned back then and let a great sigh. He looked down and his fingers turned idly around a brass button.

"I think I understand what you mean," I said.

"When you return home try to retain that understanding and impart it to others; at least make them know that something of great importance is occurring down here." Then he looked up and smiled wistfully. "Yes, you can see that I'm a school teacher, hungry for a pupil." He stood up. He was a fine-looking man, tall and lean, a quiet dignity in his comportment.

Just then we heard some commotion in the woods. It was a woman's voice, loud and unappeasable. When she appeared, bursting out of the woods via a narrow path, she was in the company of a soldier who, by his gestures, appeared to be trying to placate her and, by the tragicomical despair of these gestures, not having much success. When she saw Captain Morris she rushed past the soldier with renewed vigor and came toward us, lifting her arm and pointing a goodly finger's-worth of accusation: a short thick woman, rather round, in middle-age, a white apron tied around her, flapping as she hurried.

"Captain!" she shouted from fifty feet away, startling everyone, marching forward. "In the beginning you took our food and then our stock and then chopped down our trees, and if you'll recollect our preacher Mr. Belden warned that you would bring upon us creatures from the pits of Hades. . . ." coming toward us in this bellicose, implacable manner, toward the patient, waiting captain whose partially amused, partially concerned eyes studied her. When she arrived face to face with him he raised his hand.

"Calm yourself, Mrs. Viller," he said.

"Claims she saw a ghost," the soldier, following behind, said, shrugging expressively, prepared, apparently, to accept the ghost as he had doubtless been accepting one untoward thing after another since being in the Army, in the war.

"On horseback," Mrs. Viller said emphatically.

"In flowing white," the soldier volunteered, shrugging again.

"You've brought the devil's curse upon our land," the excited woman said. "You and your men."

"Please, calm yourself," the Captain said.

"A ghost, Captain," the soldier volunteered again, with mock seriousness this time, offering a generous wink of his eye.

"Tell us what happened, Mrs. Viller," the Captain said.

"This morning, just after sunup," Mrs. Viller said, furious and intimidated both, at the same moment, in the same tone of voice, "just as we in all our God-fearing innocence had left our beds and had finished our breakfasts and given grace to God and were beginning to go to our chores: my husband and two sons were going to the fields and my daughter to the well for water, and the old folks, my aged father and mother, in their God-fearing harmlessness, had just come out from their cabin and were walking across the yard near the haystack—when suddenly from out of the morning air we heard this soft roaring. My husband stopped and turned his head and said that it sounded like something on horseback, but my oldest boy said No, that nothing on horseback could move that fast or make that roar. Then we saw it whizzing on the other side of the alders. Then it came through the alders with the loudest smashing, all the dead twigs splitting and flying out in front of it and we saw this enormous horse with the most enormous white teeth seething and I knew that here was the devil's work at last as Preacher Belden had warned us it would come. The horse came straight through the yard. My husband and the two boys scattered, the pipe flying out of my husband's mouth and my husband moving twenty feet before the pipe touched ground; my daughter froze by the well and Ma and Pa just stiffened up like wood as this horse—big as a locomotive—flew past them. And sitting on it was the most terrifying sight a God-fearing mortal eye ever did behold."

"What was it?" the Captain asked gravely, folding his arms, prepared to receive the awesome impact of this tale.

"A man, a devil, all in white, sitting forward, his eyes glaring in his head like they had just seen all the fires of hell. He threw a cloud of dust over us all. And then he let the awfullest shriek you ever heard on God's earth."

"Shriek?" the Captain asked.

"Yes. Shriek," the woman said, her own eyes wide and shining. "Just as he went into the haystack; the horse never turned an inch, but went right into it, and I thanked God later that it wasn't our house because nothing mortal or man-made could have stopped that horse. The horse and the shriek went straight into the hay and came right out, the shriek louder and more ungodly than before, the horse smashing through so fast that you could see daylight between the top and the bottom of the haystack, the rest of it flying over the yard like in a March wind. Then they went over the rail fence by twenty feet, the horse and the man in white and the shriek, and struck the ground with thunder and kept going across the meadow with the shriek still flying out ahead of them like an unholy path they were going to take, going at such hopeless speed until the cedar the other side of the field exploded with them and finally swallowed the whole thing. Then I fainted. I'd never fainted before in my life. But I fainted then. I fainted for an hour, the blood gone completely out of my body for one whole hour—that's the kind of shock it was. When I saw light again I told them I was coming here to tell you, to tell you what you and your soldiers had wrought upon God-fearing people. My husband said that it had been a youth in underwear sitting a runaway horse—you see what it's already begun to do to people's minds."

The Captain turned to me. "Sounds like your friend," he said. The woman shot me a horrified look that made me feel the horns standing up on my forehead.

"What happened to the fellow in white?" I asked her.

"He kept going, bringing the devil's curse to the whole countryside," she said.

"He couldn't have got far there," the Captain said to me. "That's a difficult forest there, lots of tangled underbrush and second growth."

We—the Captain and I—rode out to Mrs. Viller's farm, riding along the route of the telegraph wires.

"He's probably lying out there in the forest somewhere," the Captain said.

"He has a great capacity for survival," I said.

Pointing to the wires that stretched along overhead with us, the Captain said, "Along here is where they did their deviltry last week." A few of the poles had been chopped down but others had been risen in their places, the fallen ones still lying where they had broken the undergrowth.

"Do you think they're still about?" I asked.

"Of course. It's very important to them that they nip these wires."

"Do you ever catch them?"

"We haven't yet. But we have some additional cavalry with us now, and they're on the Rebels' heels. There's all kinds of problems for us here. Being behind the lines is not as leisurely and enviable a business as it seems. For one thing, most of the people down here are against us, and although we get accustomed to that eventually, still it gives you an uncomfortable feeling. Then there's this business of tracking down deserters. They're always trying to slip back up North. Sometimes they can be as savage and dangerous as the Rebels, for they're men absolutely without honor. They know that if we catch them it means the firing squad. And they deserve it too. Deserters are the worst kind. Not only do they put an added burden on the rest, but they go back North and spread the most damnable and fallacious stories about the Army and spread other tales about the futility of the war."

"Do you ever catch them?" I asked.

"Occasionally. Sometimes they resist to an extent that we have to draw our weapons on them. We've killed several of them. But they're cunning, and murderous. They'll kill you for your money or your clothing."

We galloped down the road toward the Viller farm, passing a close forest of dead and tangled trees, mostly scrub oak, their density laced and overhung with surly looking vines.

When we reached the Viller farm we found the menfolk sitting in the yard around the ruin of their haystack. The hay had been flung a considerable distance around the yard, attesting to the velocity of Pete and Mark and the shriek.

"Which way did he go?" the Captain asked from the saddle.

The farmer stood up and with the stem of his pipe indicated a point beyond the meadow.

"Have you gone to look for him?"

The farmer shook his head vigorously.

"Have you any idea how far he went?" Captain Morris asked.

Another emphatic shake of the head. Then a stern, proud, disapproving look from beady, gray eyes.

"All right," the Captain said. We rode out into the meadow toward the cedars. At the forest's edge we dismounted. We could see where the brush had been smashed. Entering the forest, the Captain said, "Well, he couldn't have gone too far in here." It was quite dense in here, and Mark had plowed a trail that was easy to follow—flattened bushes and broken branches. Seeing the closeness of the forest I began to feel an uneasiness concerning Pete's welfare. I envisioned the Captain having to shoot poor Mark and then burying Pete out here in the forest where he had fallen.

But one half of these fears was soon allayed when, coming to a slight clearing, we saw Mark standing placidly, swinging his long face inquiringly through the high grass. He appeared quite placid, quite content, and I was certain that this satisfaction stemmed from his having successfully killed Pete Mariah.

"There's our locomotive," the Captain said. "I guess we'll find the engineer somewhere close by."

We went through the grass and I went up to Mark and took his bit and ran my hand soothingly down his face. A breeze came soughing through the trees then and it seemed to be carrying some rather offensive odor. The Captain sniffed it repellently.

"Dung," he said.

Then Pete spoke out, from some hidden place in the grass.

"Yes," his voice said. "Dung. He carried me through hell and high water and haystacks for a thousand miles but had the consideration to leave me in a soft place."

We went through the grass and there he was, sitting there with pieces of hay pasted all over his tattered long johns, sitting in a pile that his hurtling body had smashed into a new, malodorous freshness.

CHAPTER 8

1

Pete sat the rest of the day in unbecoming moroseness. His embarrassment was enormous. Not only had he let his horse carry him away (the cavalrymen in particular gave him a good time of raillery over this), but he had had to endure it all in his underwear, finally culminating the ignoble with the ignominious—sitting in a pile of horse flop. When he was brought into the camp, Captain Morris ordered him to give himself a good hard scrubbing. Then the Captain gave him a suit of old clothes which Pete gratefully put his arms and legs into. Then he told some of the soldiers—the more gullible ones—the harrowing story of his ride, of all the dangers that had kept flying up at him at every turn (he was impressed by the idea that at least one person had thought he was a ghost, and so he told of others who "must have thought the same thing, because there was a couple of them come running out of their houses and threw pitchforks at me as I put ten feet of daylight between their fencetop and my horse's underside"). Sturdy oak branches had snapped off against his shoulders and stone walls had crumbled before Mark's driving chest and a forty-foot span of swirling water had been swept by Mark's stretching body in "the greatest leap a horse, and a non-jumper at that, ever took." But he wouldn't talk about the shriek at all, except to say that it must have been one of the women on the farm that let it, because "it was only a haystack that I was about to go through."

Then, after leaving the soldiers, came the solemn part of the affair, the non-embroidered, non-embellished part. Attired in baggy brown trousers and a multicolored flannel shirt, his hair turned all askew as it ever was, Pete came up to me and asked me to accompany him into the woods. When we had got sufficiently out of sight we stopped amid some blackberry bushes and he looked at me.

"Jeff," he said (and when he said Jeff and not Deacon I knew that his heart was really in what he was going to say and so I forbade myself even the merest twinkle of levity). "You got to promise me one thing before we go on."

"What's that?" I asked.

A pained look crossed his face. But he went on. "You got to promise that when we get back to Capstone you'll regard this as too infamous a misfortune to talk about."

"I would never tell anyone," I said. "You know that."

"Mark was scared by the shot. I couldn't do anything but sit it out."

"You did as well as any man could," I said.

He gave me his hand. We shook solemnly.

"You're a true friend, Deacon," he said.

* * *

The next morning Captain Morris gave us each a haversack of food and gave Pete a new pipe and gave us both some tobacco, and along with all that he gave us some pretty precise instructions.

"I want you boys to turn around right here and begin heading back to New York," he said. "If you find yourselves continuing to dream about the South then in a year or so you can join the Army and come down here under more legitimate circumstances."

"Yes sir," I said. But the way he looked at me made me feel as if he had seen right through my lie (I always found it the most difficult thing to lie to someone that I liked), that he knew we were going to go on, and that there was indeed some reason, some important reason, that we could not impart to him. So he said,

"If you're found down here again I'll see to it that you're put under arrest."

"We won't be found," I said.

The Captain gave Charl a slap across the rump and we rode off, going back up the road, moving at a brisk canter.

"I reckon he knows you lied about going back," Pete said.

"Doesn't make that much difference," I said. "If we get caught again it's unlikely that it will be by him. I figure we've got at least a dozen more second chances to use up before we hit any real trouble."

"But suppose it's Rebels the next time?"

"Then we've got Uncle Clay's pistols," I said.

The morning was gray, chilly. We could smell rain coming. The woods did not come awake this morning, the gray pall glooming them with a deep, somber stillness. We listened to the soft, constant clopclop struck by our horses, passing the silent birdless trees that seemed to be regarding us as some part of the death that was in descent upon them, our clopclop striking dully through the still, empty, shedding trees like a hostile edict. Winter's approach was clearly over the woods, even where the trees still held their colorful blaze of leaves. The deeper the wood went the darker and gloomier it became until it seemed to contain a soul deep within itself, deep within the sorrowing, unanswering trees. The sun would not appear, we cast no shadows, moving on past all the gloomy dying like interlopers.

Then the rain began, seemed to emerge from its suspension in the gray misty air. We heard it in the woods first, ticking on the dead leaves. Then it was in our faces, slow and cold. It remained a very light rain, hanging a thin, gray, patient curtain around us, beginning to darken the rocks in the road, covering them drop by drop until the rocks were dark; falling steadily into the roadside brush, making the leaves quiver.

"Maybe we ought to start cutting around," I said. "This road leads straight north."

"We'll have to take a pretty wide swing around if we're going to avoid those soldiers," Pete said.

"Baker Station is southwest of here. We can get a good start on it from the other side of this timber."

"Suppose we see some soldiers?"

"We'll outrun them this time," I said.

We cut off of the road and began picking our way through the wood. There was not so much undergrowth here and we were able to travel unimpeded. Riding through the woods we could hear the rain but did not very much feel it, but the gray mist was all about us, webbing the trees, creating a lonely and forlorn impression of a journey deep into some bleak and unchartered wilderness. Our pace was necessarily slow, our noises lost in the steady overhead cadence of rain. I closed my collar with my fingertips and held it shut by putting my chin down. In the wood, in the slow, gray rain, I began to feel a great hollowness inside of me, a feeling of lostness and abandonment, a conscious awareness that I was far away from my home where now the fire was red in the hearth and even if it was raining on the fields at least they were my fields and I could run through them to where the fire was and warm food and dry socks; for the loneliness, the strangeness, overhung this dismal place like a shroud: and my eyes, downcast in the effort to keep my collar closed, were watching the minute procession of moistened foliage and the slow dutiful strides of Charl's forelegs as they paced the dark earth: and I remembered Pa saying, You have never been away from home before, and what he had meant when he said it, and thinking the vague thought that not far away men were dying here in woods like these and above it all there seemed something so vast and powerful and lamentable that it was impossible to reconcile it with human understanding. And then I sought to think—How childish it is to think of your home when you are away from it—and sought to bolster and embolden myself by belittling my loneliness, by trying to remember all the times I had sat home and wished that I were here where I now was, trying to recapture for reality the bold and audacious spirit that animates imagination.

Then from behind came a sound from Pete and my eyes came up. Over a fall of green plumage that hung over our trail, I saw something that froze me—something that my credulity was going to have to separate from illusion before I could become afraid. Ahead, beyond the gateway of leaves, in a small clearing, a Confederate soldier was sitting his horse. Seen through the fine rain-mist, a thicket of sky-pointing pine behind him, he looked unreal, like a piece of equestrian sculpture left behind to the wilderness, turning grayer and grayer in the fine, slow-falling rain. He neither saw nor heard us. He was sitting in profile to us, erect and alert in his saddle, a long straight nose and then long, sad beard under his slouch hat. One hand rested on the pommel. The more we gazed at him the larger he seemed to become, sitting alone heroic and symbolic in the mist awaiting his summons. So intense and immutable was his gaze that we were compelled to follow its direction, certain that some awesome spectacle lay within it. But we saw nothing except the clearing and then the pines the other side of it, everything still and dreary in the sad gray rain that continued slowly and interminably over the woods. And then we realized. He was listening. He and the great horse—they were a single figure now, as if eternally inseparable, one graced and balanced by the other—the horse aware and sensitive to the rider's thoughts and instincts; they would think and act as one; the horse with the rider's divination, the rider with the horse's strength and dash.

And then, even before there was motion anywhere, before a blade of grass had trembled, we could see it happening, beginning; the animation beginning to pour in him; even before he moved a muscle it was surging in his body and through him like an electric current into his horse; making him even taller and larger in the gray mist-rain: because he heard it first, took it out of the air just a fraction of a second before we did—what he had been waiting for, known was coming: the sound of men in the woods. Then he whirled, his horse rising on its hind legs for an instant as if to make a grand and glorious beginning, the soldier tilted back through the air, the reins suddenly appearing taut in his hand, his legs holding fast to the animal's flanks; whirling so quickly and moving so quickly (it seemed that the moment the horse's hoofs touched the ground they were in full gallop, as if they had been galloping for miles, they had that same stunning propulsion) and suddenly so surging and alive and inevitable it seemed he had never been standing still (we never knew, could never determine, later, how long we had sat watching him), and coming in a rush through the mist, loud and terrible and enormous, generating a terrific seething; right through the brush with an explosion and past us by several feet, his eyes throwing us a wild unhuman glare like the fixed eyes in the paintings of mythical giants, looking at us but not seeing us, but we seeing him down to the very last detail: the color of his eyes, the long uncurved nose, the mouth opened in a black shoutless orifice through the beard, his body beginning to bend forward, his back arcing: the horse storming past with wind and noise through the brush, its breast smashing everything before it; and then he was past us, we were too terrified to see where, for we could begin to see the others dimly through the pines, a moving, shaping mass, hear their voices.

"Pete!" I said, dismounting. I led Charl by the bit into a thicket and there induced him to lie down behind the moldy, moss-covered trunk of a fallen tree; Pete right behind, having a bit more difficulty with Mark but finally getting him down too, the great horse sitting itself awkwardly and unwillingly on its hind legs and then Pete tugging it down the rest of the way, the two of us lying in amidst the hard-breathing, startled horses, peering breathlessly through the thicket's tangled undergrowth.

It sounded like a dozen horsemen but when we saw them there were only four. When they came out of the wood they galloped across the clearing and we were able to hear their voices.

"I saw him!" one cried. "He went through here somewhere!"

They paused at just the point where the Rebel had ridden through. I could see them through the thicket—four Union cavalrymen, poised in the misty rain on wet-glistening horses, poised and restive and eager.

"I don't hear anything in there," one said.

"He might have dismounted."

"Let's spread out and try and flush him."

One voice, sterner and quicker than the others—the one in authority apparently—snapped out several brisk instructions, the most chilling being (and he issued it in the same tone of voice as the rest, as if it were the same as the rest) that if the Rebel resisted to kill him. Then they plunged in, two of them entering the wood further up, two others passing within feet of where we lay and looking up through the tree's dead branches I watched their horses file past like two gigantic craft, the letters U.S. in gold thread on the blue saddle blankets. They passed quietly, we listened to them going through the wood, listened to them and to the rain coming down just a little faster now, like myriad tiny feet scurrying lightly all over the leaves.

"Where do you think he went?" Pete whispered.

"I don't know," I whispered back, running my hand up and down Charl's face, trying to keep him still because he was restless, because he could probably sense it, the trouble, the death that had entered the woods.

We listened, listened very hard, trying to know it before it happened, frozen with frightened curiosity. From the other side we could hear the other two troopers. Their passage was evidently more difficult because we kept hearing twigs and branches breaking and the long, windlike swishing of foliage. The four troopers were circling around through the trees and the longer it took the more I thought about the Rebel, seeing again his face, feeling the frantic haste—an aura of which he had left behind him—and terror and desperation, more terror and desperation than I had ever seen before in a man and it frightened me to think that it could exist that way, that there was something in the world (and so close upon him too) to inflame and madden a man with such seizures, to quicken him with such implacable fears. I knew that he had not gone far, that he was somewhere near, the terrible animation still surging through him.

Then we heard a shout, and then a melee of several voices. There was a sudden struggle somewhere behind us. The voices were clashing and upon their frenetic excitement came a pistol shot and an even greater shouting and then the sound of a horse thundering massively through the woods. I lifted my head over the thicket and saw a horseman tearing through everything before him, and behind him I saw a pistol flash and heard the loud report, but nothing, not the wild shouting nor the yelling voices which were coming from all around could stop him. He tore past us, just over where we were hiding and I saw, or rather remembered, two things: his body bent so low on the horse that his beard seemed to be flying out of the horse's fluttering mane; and the fresh blood gleaming in the long, red slashes that thorns had ripped across the horse's heaving flanks. The horse leaped and the brush flew open against the gray sky and horse and rider poured through the great fanlike opening. As the brush swept back shut again he was galloping across the clearing, whizzing through the slanting rain, dashing into the trees on the other side.

The Union troopers were yelling. It seemed like a thousand of them. Two emerged from the other side of the wood and galloped across the clearing parallel to where we lay and I had only a quick glimpse of the two troopers leaning forward in their saddles, flashing through the rain. Then the other two came on, pasing us, one holding a pistol up in his hand, jouncing in his saddle, his horse sailing with abrupt and stunning grace over several fallen trees and bounding into the clearing with its rider yelling: "Get him! Get him! Get him!"—the voice sounding wild and insane, shouting off into the rain. The fourth rider came through at another point, racing through the rain with a certain eagerness and vexation —at being last, probably. Then all four had swept over the grassy clearing and disappeared into the woods. We could hear the shouting and then the pistol again and then other pistols and the horses rushing through the trees with a strange, dark unseen power.

"They'll get him sure," Pete said.

"I hope they stay on the other side of that clearing," I said, shifting about, trying to see through the thicket, holding tightly to Charl's bit now, trying to soothe him with my other hand.

We could see them galloping through the pines, great vague shadows flitting about, the yelling going on as though they were trying to shout their quarry into submission. Then there was a particularly piercing yelling and a burst of gunfire like grounded thunder in the woods, and all the voices thronged together in a yelling that sounded like panic but which was surprise and maybe even desperation, and we saw what it was all about in a moment when the Rebel came through the trees, the brush smashing open before him, his horse in full gallop, its head held up so that you could see its eyes gleaming; coming through the rain like that in desperation's final headlong rush, the soldier crouched on the horse in galvanized intensity, having turned and twisted through the wood and outmaneuvered his tormentors and now making his final, fateful dash; himself and his horse pitted against earth and time and the willful indiscriminations of fortune: the wood behind him thrashing with pounding horses and throbbing with yelling, and then the gunshots, and even before the shots overtook him he seemed doomed because his desperation was too much, he wanted too badly to succeed, because his soul was importuning, and because of the gray mournful rain which seemed intent upon washing a corpse this morning.

I could not see the Union troopers and the chances were that they could not see the Rebel and were shooting at the noise. He was hit just as he had made little more than half the clearing. The bullets made him shudder and come stiffly erect for the moment, his rising hands losing the reins as he began to sit taller and taller in the saddle, even his head coming up until his beard was sticking out straight and his hat was floating behind him and one hand was opened flat against his breast. He started to fall, tilting off to one side as stiff as a block of wood and his fall seemed incredibly deliberate as if he were dismounting at his ease; he became suspended in the air in an almost horizontal position, until the frantic horse, in frenzied gallop, threw him and he tipped way out and plunged toward the fleeing ground like a falling oar toward water, striking the ground and then bouncing up several feet, reappearing exactly as he had fallen—hand still flat upon breast, face unchanged. But then he twisted and whirled and slammed again upon the ground, still even with the frantic horse and we saw then that one foot was caught in the stirrup and the horse was sweeping and dragging and whirling him along. His hands flew out as his body performed another helpless sickening whirl and thud and whirl again, sweeping through the grass in a wild violent mowing. Then the horse was at the edge of the clearing and the soldier threw a crooked arm over his face as the horse whipped him into the thicket and then into the fallen trees with a mighty thud and he flew up again, arms and legs all flying freely now, whirling—his head went through his ankles for a moment—and then he crashed and remained as the horse went on into the woods as if to become a ghost, a legend.

The Union troopers came through the clearing then, the four of them, appearing with uniform suddenness as though they had just charged off a pedestal. They came thundering through the wood in pursuit of the riderless horse, thundering and rattling and crashing, each alert and lusty, their horses springing with magnificent strides, the woods shattering before them. And then they were gone and it was finished, the mighty dream vanished in a terrifying sweep as the murmurous sorrow fell upon the end of violence and filtered through the trees in ancient grieving.

We waited for awhile in the thicket. We couldn't see the Rebel soldier but we could hear the harsh gasps of his breathing. He seemed to be in an agonizing struggle for the fulfillment of some cherished peace he suddenly realized did exist; his breathing noisy, collapsing in empty shatterings and then gathering and rising again, progressively weaker and weaker. We began to realize that the Union troopers were not coming back, that they were going to be chasing the riderless horse for some time.

When we stood up we saw him. He was lying on his back upon the broken branches at the thicket's edge, one arm flung out, his other hand gathered against himself at the beltline, the fingers smeared and sticky-looking with blood. His uniform was ripped and torn badly in many places. He was lying heavily, seemingly immovable, showing how he had struck the ground with terrific impact, his body numb and helpless with shock. He was gazing up toward the sky, his eyes thin, tragic. His faint, difficult breaths rippled down through his beard. For a few minutes his eyes did not appear to know that we were there, resting hypnotically upon the gray sky, until finally they let go of the sky and moved to us, fixing upon us flat and gray and already beginning to glaze over.

"We want to help you," I said.

But he did not speak. His eyes were stuck to my face. He was dying. I could tell it then. It was all gone from his body, the fear and the desperation and the surging importance of everything, all gone as if it had never been, or had never really mattered, and he was watching me as if to see where it had gone, his eyes receding imperceptibly further and further from me, their gaze unchanging, mute and tragic and unblinking.

"There must be something we can do," Pete whispered.

The rain fell softly on the dying man, coming through the trees in a light, steady streaming, the little dark spots appearing on the torn uniform. And all through the woods the rain created a sad, sobbing quiet. His face—in strange, mystic opposition to the uniform which in appearance still bespoke of unregenerative violence and fever and passion—his face filled with a deep, solemn peace.

"Do you want some water?" I asked.

His hand moved, uncovering his wound, showing it to us. The bullet had torn clean through him, coming out just over the beltline. His hand lifted for a moment over the wound, as if to show us how simple it was, and hopeless, and foolish. Then his hand covered the wound again. And then I realized I was looking into the eyes of a dead man, because the breathing was gone, and I didn't know for how long it had been, and I knew that my face had been the last thing on this earth that he had seen.

I looked at Pete. "He's dead," I said.

"Yes," Pete said.

We looked down at the calm, still face, at the eyes which

had ceased to be eyes now, their staring a nothingness, an empty dialogue between soul and sky.

"I wonder who he was," I said.

"A soldier."

"I'm glad we didn't kill him," I said.

"Those soldiers killed him," Pete said.

"I know."

All over the wood, upon every leaf, we could hear the rain, sad and constant and mysterious.

We had nothing with which to dig a grave, so we covered him as best we could with leaves and branches, hoping that someone would find him later, or if not then in the spring, and give him a decent burial.

Then we mounted our horses and went on, through the clearing into the woods again.

2

So that was war, and now I had been part of it. I wondered if all men felt as I did now, old and tired under the burden of melancholy sadness, of helplessness, of a peculiar wisdom that did not enlighten or impale any areas of darkness, but which simply broadened and deepened the quest, opened new areas of unknowing.

I tried not to think of the dead soldier, but it was impossible, and so I tried to concentrate on the fact that he had been an enemy and would have killed me if he had been given the chance. But that was no good either because I couldn't equivocate a human being just to accommodate my sorrow; there was no justification for callousness, for treating death so lightly, and I thought of battles in which a thousand men die, or five thousand men, but still that did not diminish nor lessen the significance of the death of the one man.

Pete rode behind in silence. We were like a two-man funeral procession threading our way through the trees, the shadows flicking off us (for the sun had begun to break through now, the rain gone, and we had not even noticed it); inarticulate with grief, with puzzlement. I felt as though the Rebel had been a lifelong friend, that I had known him and his wife and family, and I thought of his wife sitting somewhere in South Carolina (for I decided that that was his home) thinking of him and writing him a letter telling him to take care of himself and to be careful, and that Pete and I were the only ones in the world who knew that he was dead, and I wished that I could someday after the war go to his wife and tell her how he had died. Thinking all of these things as gradually the rain stopped and the clouds broke and the sun began to drift hazily through the woods. And then Pete saying,

"All right. Suppose he would have cut the wires. That could've cost more lives than his—plenty more."

"Sure," I said.

"So stop mourning. We'll probably see a lot more of that before we're through down here."

I whirled around. "Shut up!" I said. "Just you shut up!"

The rain didn't stop until early afternoon, having continued steadily the whole time we were riding through the wood. Then it had stopped and slanting pillars of cloudy sunlight began appearing all around us. A blue sky covered the treetops, a bright clear blue, marked with cozy white clouds. A cool breeze began when we finally emerged from the wood and trotted down an old dirt road that ran along the fields of an abandoned farm. The wind slipped in soft rushes through the grass and into the wood and the wood began its own rain. The wind was sailing through the trees and catching the branches and each wetted leaf was rolling drops of rain down upon other branches and other leaves and we heard the rain all over again as we rode in yellow sunlight under the blue sky. The wind became stronger and the branches shook harder and the wetted leaves went from trembling to waving and the silver rain-specks fell faster and all through the woods came the strange, sourceless noise of fallen rain falling again and it was as haunting as a dream.

CHAPTER 9

We rode all afternoon without seeing anyone. The countryside had been abandoned. The few farms we passed were deserted. The closer we were coming to the armies the more leaden, more ominous the world seemed to be getting. War was casting its reign of gloom, a dark, low, palpable cloud.

Sometimes I moved Charl at a gallop, watching the road roll up at me, watching the cool wind swirl the dead leaves about in wild scatterings of color. Then I would bring him back to a trot. Once we paused at a stream and let the horses drink, Charl nuzzling daintily at the purling water while I stroked his long, bent neck. Looking up beyond the treetops I saw the wind riding the clouds, long and thin now, across the declining blue. Then we rode again and the wind continued to feel good, cleansing the air, changing it, changing everything in a bold, mighty sweep.

At dusk we halted and prepared to make camp. With the sun's departure the air began turning chilly. We tethered the horses and went looking for some dry wood. We finally found some fence rails that had collapsed and been partially covered by some bramble and, carrying them back on our shoulders, we broke them up and were able to make a fire with them. We put Captain Morris' haversacks to good use then, taking out coffee and hardtack and bacon and a tin of beans, cooking everything carefully and eating slowly, making of it a grand meal; after which we sat back and smoked our pipes, keeping the fire going. Darkness came quickly, building the surrounding woods into a great wall.

"You know," I said—and the way I said it, quiet and reflective, I guess I had been thinking about it without knowing—"that captain was a pretty good fellow. We did some talking. He was a school teacher before the war. He was telling me about why the war was being fought, what all is at stake and what it means and what it does to men."

"School teachers can tell you things," Pete said.

"But he made sense," I said. "He explained how the whole country would fall apart if we lost the war. And how the country was such a young country and how it had to live. And he said how war could corrupt a man's scruples and turn him out to be something nature never intended him for."

"I don't know," Pete said, staring vaguely. "He might be right. But I sometimes think men are what they are."

"Yes, but a war will bring out the worst."

"It's supposed to, isn't it, if a man is to be an effective soldier?"

"But war opens up emotions in a man that he can't just turn off that easily. A man shouldn't be faced with an opening up of those emotions. It's bad for him, bad for the country later on. And the country has got to remain strong after the war is over."

It was a strange, new feeling. It seemed to be all around, alive and alert; quick in the earth, present in the trees, flowing and soaring upward to the sky. I felt the Captain's words now in warm firm impact. I had seen a man die in the context of those words. And not far away were thousands of other men who would die for the "deep historical purpose." The Captain's words fell around my shoulders now like a mantle, a warm flag. It became a deepening and inspiriting sensation—being suddenly a part of the fight for the country, the survival. It was a feeling of vast encompassment, as though something great and transcendent had reached down and gathered my derelict and uncomprehending soul, and not from pity or anger or malice, but because I was needed, because I could contribute.

I took out the map and opened it up. The fire ran red shadows over its worn and well-folded surface.

"We should be nearing the Potomac in a day or two," I said. "Once we get across we should be able to reach Baker Station with a day's ride."

"Suppose Clay's not there?"

"We'll wait on him," I said.

"How about those other places Alamine Johnson mentioned?"

"They're too far south. Some of them are behind the Rebel lines."

"Behind their lines? Clay sure takes chances, don't he?"

I folded the map, the quarters falling right over into the deep, accustomed folds, and put it away inside my shirt.

"He's not afraid of anything," I said absently, hardly aware that I was saying it. Maybe it was because I was tired, or maybe because so much had happened during the past few days, but I did not feel the warmth and animation I had always felt when talking about Uncle Clay. He seemed a remote figure. I sat stubbornly, not saying any more about him, not thinking of him.

"I've never been in Virginia," Pete said. "I wonder what it's like."

"Well, you'd never been in Pennsylvania or Maryland either before, and you don't look any different for having been there."

"That's right. I reckon Virginia oughtn't be much different from here. We're only crossing a river, not an ocean."

"It's more than just a river now," I said. "It's one hell of a lot more than that. We'll have to be less trustful of whoever we meet from now on. We won't be able to trust anybody. And nobody will be trusting us."

"We'll have to sleep one eye at a time," Pete said.

"You sorry you came along, Deacon?" I asked him.

"No, Deacon," he said. "I'm not one hundred per cent joyful, but I'm not sorry either. There's not much doing back in Capstone now. They're all getting fixed to dig in for the winter, for a long snooze by the fireside. I know my people are. What do you think your Pa's doing?"

"He's waiting for me to get back."

"I hope he doesn't get impatient, not that George Adamson would be much of a loss to the community."

"Pa won't get impatient," I said.

"Does he have any idea who you're after down here?"

"No."

"Rachel won't tell him either, will she?"

"Let's leave off of that, say, Pete?" I said testily. "Let's just leave Capstone where it is."

"All right," Pete said, shrugging. "Just trying to liven up the evening. Don't know what you're so riled up about anyway. Hell, I've got five sisters. . . ."

We put some more wood on the fire and drew in closer to it. It crackled quietly, fierce and independent. Pete lapsed into silence. It wore badly on him because he was such an inveterate jabberer. But I let it hang for awhile, and then I started in to feel lonely.

"A fire always looks like more than it really is," I said. "It looks like it knows all the secrets and all the answers."

"You just give it a chance," Pete said, "and it'll show you what it knows. It knows how to eat up this whole end of the country if you let it."

"Oh it can do that all right. But look at it now." We watched it. Out there in the lonely countryside it had an uncanny hypnotic effect, as if trying to draw us under its spell, its lusty little flames darting and lunging. "But then look at it in the morning," I said. "Nothing but cold ashes. You can sift them all day and not find a thing. It's all gone. The fire is gone, taking everything with it. Where does it go?"

"Please, please, Deacon," Pete said puffing on his pipe. "These kind of speculations are bad for the brain."

I smiled self-consciously.

"A fire is nothing but a fire," Pete said, putting in the last word. "It can't be eaten or worn or pressed between the pages of a book. So leave it at that."

We sat back quietly then, smoking our pipes, our eyes

roving through the dark, the shadows; detached from each other now in one of the curious intervals during which men will drift apart from each other into their own intimate secrecies, our thoughts carrying us wide and far, into dreams and desires and into the unillumined plains of the unknown.

But what my exact thoughts were then I don't remember. They must have been vague and far and quite consuming, because I don't remember hearing anyone approach, I don't remember first seeing anyone—that is, not the suddenness of seeing, of seeing the person whole and complete; but rather it was gradual, like a revelation; the face emerging from the darkness as if the moving shadows were shaping it, with each lunge and flicker adding another lineament until it was there staring at me, eyes and nose and mouth and long beardless jaw; and then the features, like things taking shape as reality begins to harden itself, beginning to appear with each expression intact and finalized: the firelight reflecting a malevolent gleaming in the eyes, the nose long and sloping, the mouth arranged in a sardonically amused smirk, and the long down-jutting jaw that looked like an elbow; and then the uniform—the blue forage cap rakishly to a side, and the coat with the sergeant's stripes on one sleeve and one gold button dangling loosely and the mud-caked trousers that rose up from the bush and became the man.

We stared at each other, like man and alter ego, like soul and ghost; he sardonic and aware, I intrigued and not believing, watching the shadows run over him like black water; and then his smile opened and his white teeth showed slowly and I knew then that he was really there.

"Pete," I said

Holding his pipe in his mouth with his hand, Pete looked across at me, his eyes sleepy.

"We've got company," I said.

He turned around with a start, pipe in hand now.

The person emerged from the shadows, walking slowly in toward the fire. He was a very tall man, perhaps four inches over six feet. Looking up at him from my sitting position it was as if one of the trees had suddenly come to life and was striding toward me. Then he stopped, the smile, the smirk, continuing on his face.

"We saw your fire," he said.

The "we" made me look beyond him toward the trees. There was someone else there but I was unable to distinguish who, or how many, they were.

"We figured you was Christian folk and wouldn't mind sharing your fire, and maybe a bit of grub," he said.

"Of course not," I said. "You're welcome here, you and your friend. . . ."

"Friends," he said. He turned around, his great head twisting on his neck. "Abel," he said. "It's all right. These young fellers are right hospitable."

There was a light snapping in the brush and two more figures began to materialize. One was another Union soldier, a rather small man, rather shabby-looking, not at all much like a soldier, wearing a derby which made him and his uniform appear ludicrous. With him was a young girl, of our own age, or maybe a year more. Pete and I rose at the sight of her. She followed the small soldier. He was leading her by the hand. She seemed quite timid and unwilling, her face tense with fear and grief. But she was very pretty, I could see that even through the dirt smudges on her face and even though her long, black hair hung loose and uncombed over her shoulders. She was wearing a man's coat over a white blouse and what appeared to be a man's work pants. Alighting upon me, her eyes filled with a tragic appeal that sent a peculiar warm shudder through me.

"That's the good girl," the tall one said, watching them come up to the fire. He reached out and mussed her hair as her head jerked back away. He laughed. Then he turned back to us.

"That's Barbie," he said. "She's most shy."

We nodded to her, Pete trying to smooth back his hair.

"I reckon we all got names," the tall one said, still smirking through his teeth, first to Pete then to me.

"Jeff," I said.

"Pete Mariah," Pete said, addressing the girl.

"Sergeant John Sleavey," the tall one said. "New York Volunteers. My small friend here is Private Abel Pierce—doesn't know whether he's from Vermont or New Hampshire."

"Vermont," the small one said churlishly.

"It's Vermont now, is it?" Sleavey asked. "Well, it's all the same I suppose. It's not where you're from but where you're going that counts, eh, boys?"

"You're welcome to some coffee and hardtack," I said.

"Coffee and hardtack, eh?" Sleavey said. "You fellers ain't Army by any chance?"

"No," I said.

"That's right. You're too young."

"We're just passing through," I said.

"Well it's a good country to be passing through," Sleavey said. He crouched and helped himself to some coffee. He drank from Pete's cup, draining it in two quick gulps, then handed some hardtack into his mouth and chewed voluminously for a moment, then expectorated distastefully. He looked up and smirked a semblance of apology. "No reflection, sonny," he said. "But I hate hardtack." Then he stood up, hitching his trousers with his thumbs. "Yep, a good country to be passing through, but a mighty poor one to be stopping in, right, Abel?"

"Would you like some coffee?" I asked the girl.

"Sure, Barbie," Sleavey said. "Have some coffee. She's traveled a long ways today." But the girl didn't move, her hand still attached to the small soldier's. "Fact is," Sleavey said, "we've all traveled a long ways. Those your horses, boys?"

"That's right," I said.

"Fine-looking animals."

Pete moved around away from him and we stood together. Sleavey surveyed us with sly, musing interest, like some giant about to gorge a meal.

"My, but we've had hard luck," he said. "Separated from our company like we was. Mighty hard luck. Skirmish at one of the fords yesterday morning and lots of confusion and me and Abel found ourselves lost. So we're heading up here looking for the Army. Haven't seen any Union soldiers, have you, boys?"

"Not since this morning," I said.

"Well that's a shame, a real shame." He crouched again and opened his hands over the dying fire.

"The Army is south of here," Pete said. "You're heading north."

"Do tell?" Sleavey said. "Hear that, Abel?" he said, opening and closing his huge hands low over the fire. "We been traveling in the wrong direction. I suppose you boys wouldn't want to sell us those horses of yours."

"We need them," I said.

"We'd give a fair price."

"We need them."

"Where you boys from anyway?"

"New York."

"New York you say? Well, we're neighbors."

The small one came closer, still pulling the girl whose eyes still watched me, still consumed with fear, still appealing.

"I've got some bacon in my haversack," I said, stepping back. I went to where the horses were in the trees. It was dark there, beyond the fire's fall. I opened the saddlebag and took out both of Uncle Clay's pistols, stuffing them into my shirt and closing my coat over them. Then I came away from the trees, back into the firelight. The haversack was lying there and I tried to appear surprised that it was there and I opened it and took out some bacon and dropped it into the pan. Sleavey was watching me carefully, a malicious little half-smile fixed on his mouth.

"We'd sure like to buy your horses," he said.

"They're not for sale," I said.

"That's a pity," he murmured, still crouched over the fire. Pete said, "You said there was a skirmish?"

"Oh a real bad one," Sleavey said. "Lots of men killed

Rebs all around us, hollering and shooting. A man was lucky to get away with his life."

"We can lead you back to where there's some Union cavalry," Pete said.

Sleavey's eyes came up, studying him, filled with pure malice. "Oh but you're a good feller," he said sardonically.

"I figure the Army will miss a big fellow like you," Pete said.

"Oh yes," Sleavey said. "I'm sure Gen'rl McClellan is out looking for me right now."

I pulled one of the pistols out of my shirt. Sleavey stared at me, the smirk frozen on his mouth, savage.

"You can't have our horses," I said.

"There's no call to pull a pistol on us, boy. That's not a very neighborly thing."

"I just want to make the point."

He stood up. It seemed to take him a long time to reach his height. He towered over us, watching us. He rubbed his hand down the long, knobby chin, running his tongue along the inside of his mouth.

"Well," he said, "I reckon we're not wanted here."

"I'll bet you're wanted someplace else," I said.

"We ain't deserters," Sleavey said.

"Never said you were," I said.

"Yes they are," the girl said suddenly. She broke free from the small one and ran past him and Sleavey to us. Pete grabbed her and drew her back. We were on the one side of the fire now, the two soldiers on the other. "They came to our farm this morning," the girl said, her voice running light and scared and breathless. "They clubbed my

Ma and Pa and burned the house and made me go with them. They're deserters, the both of them. Don't let them. . . ." Her voice trailed off, still scared, uncertain now.

"That's a hysterical gal that one," Sleavey said.

"I reckon you two had better back off now," I said.

"Maybe that pistol ain't as big as you think," Sleavey said, his face scowling, his voice threatening, ugly.

I showed him the other one then, holding one in each hand. He nodded, stepping back.

"This ain't neighborly at all," he murmured. "Abel," he said over his shoulder. "These folks don't want us here. I reckon we'll have to leave."

He backed away, looking at us. Gradually the shadows rose upon him, reaching higher and higher, dancing upward his face and then covering his face and he was gone, the both of them were gone, absorbed by the night shadows. We watched the darkness. Except for the patient crackling of the fire we could hear nothing. Then, out of the night, the woods, the quiet, came his voice, mild and sly and almost pleasant: "Wouldn't be surprised if we meet again, fellers. Wouldn't be at all surprised." Then we heard them going off into the wood, stealthily into the night, and gone.

The girl looked as though she couldn't believe it, and she even said it with disbelief. "They're gone."

"I only wish they were," I said, stuffing the pistols down into my belt again. "I guess we'd better move out of here. Pete."

"I hear you," he said. He went to the horses and began untying them. The girl was looking at me. She wasn't sure yet.

I asked her, "Can you sit a horse?"

"I was raised on a farm," she said.

"Is Barbie really your name?"

"Barbara."

"How long have you been with them?"

"Since this morning. They made me come with them."

"Have they . . . done anything to you?"

"No," she said, her eyes falling. "They were afraid to stop anywhere. Nightfall, they kept telling me. Nightfall. You don't know my thanks when they saw your fire. I didn't care who it was, soldiers or anybody. I was just grateful for someone, anyone. They would have killed you for those horses you know."

"They still might," I said. "If we give them that chance."

Pete came with the horses then. I stamped out the fire. The night fell over the light, the expired warmth, dark and cold.

"You can ride with me," I said. I mounted and then helped her up onto the saddle behind me. She leaned forward and wrapped her arms around my waist. I saw Pete looking at me and I guess I gave him a pretty sharp look back because he turned away and kicked at Mark and we followed him out of the wood toward the road.

Her head was pressed against my back. She was very tired I guess. I watched everything carefully as we moved down the road. I kept one hand on the butt of one of the pistols. I mistrusted every sound and shadow, everything; the kind of constant, blinkless mistrust that becomes stubborn in you when your life has become up for grabs. I knew they weren't going to give up that easily. They needed the horses. I hadn't felt it before, but now I began to feel a cold fear about Sleavey. The way he had come out of the shadows. The mere size of him. His arms—I could just see them reaching from out of the dark and sweeping us from the horse.

I had no way of knowing which way they had gone. I didn't even know for sure which way we were going, the night was impenetrable. The road wound through the woods and it was so dark that we could have been moving in circles without knowing it.

"How well do you know this country?" I asked her back over my shoulder.

"I've never been here before," she said.

I didn't say anything.

"I'm sorry," she said.

"It's all right," I said. She wrapped her arms more snugly around me and I felt like kicking Charl and making him gallop for top speed.

I wasn't sure how far Charl could go with the double load, so we halted after a little while. We went off the road into a field and dismounted there.

"I guess it's safe to stop a while," I said.

"I don't know, Deacon," Pete said. "I was trying to follow the road the best I could, and the impression I got was that we were going nowhere."

"What do you mean?"

"I think it circles through the woods and comes right back to its beginnings."

"Then there's no sense riding blind," I said. "We might as well stay here until we can get our bearings."

"No fire, right, Deacon?"

"Not even to light your pipe."

Pete moved the horses over toward the wood. He did not tether them because we might be moving out in a hurry. He stayed there with the horses, just at the edge of the wood. I thought that maybe I ought to give him one of the pistols, but I couldn't help remembering what had happened the last time he'd had a pistol in his hand.

It was getting chillier and I wished we could build a fire. I paced back and forth in the dark for a few minutes and then stopped, abruptly. I was imitating Uncle Clay again. I realized it. That was always his way when he had a problem—quick, impatient pacing as if trying to wear the problem down under his shiny, black boots, and inevitably finding the solution that way. But it wasn't my way. You can't think your own thoughts if you're walking in somebody else's footsteps. So I stopped, because I needed my own thoughts now.

She had been watching me. Standing there in the dark like a religious statue, in her man's coat and trousers, watching me. We spoke from several feet apart.

"How far do you live from here?" I asked.

"About ten miles."

"Where?"

"At a crossroads called Mardersville."

"We'll bring you back. We're heading south."

"Where are you going?"

"South," I said, curtly, tactlessly, as if she had ought not to have asked. The curt, repetitive answer stopped her for a moment. I was sorry I had said it like that. Then she said,

"I want to thank you."

"I'm sorry for what they did. I guess you're going to have a harsh impression now of our soldiers."

"They're not soldiers. Deserters aren't soldiers."

"Our soldiers don't want to be here. But it's a job. It has to be done."

"Being a soldier can change a man sometimes."

"Yes, change him maybe. Or reveal him."

"My brothers are soldiers," she said.

"Your brothers?"

"I have four. They're soldiers now, all of them. You'll say they're in the wrong army."

"If it's what they believe—"

"But it's not that. They don't believe anything. They don't care, aren't interested. They joined because they wanted to ... because they ... they joined for the wrong reasons, not to defend or uphold. They joined because they had a lust for killing. Pa said he would give one hundred dollars gold to the one that killed the most Yankees, and the oldest, Bart, said, 'Does that take in wounded and prisoners?' and Pa said that a Yankee was a Yankee. Now they're all with Lee, killing, or thinking about killing, or perhaps getting killed themselves. So when they came this morning, those two, I was almost glad they were taking me away. I was going to bed in tears every night after listening to talk of killing and killing. Every night Pa would talk of it, and before him my brothers, until the last of them had gone off. I can't stand that any more. I don't care who's right or who's wrong, but they can't go on killing like that. Doesn't God mean anything any more? Isn't there a better way? Is killing the only answer?"

We had been drawing closer as she spoke, imperceptibly,

motionlessly, as if the earth had been moving. Her face was before me. I could see into her eyes, see the grief and the concern; her eyes upon me as if I could do something about it.

"We saw a man shot this morning," I said. "He died before our eyes."

"Then you understand."

"Yes." I could feel her breathing against my face. Lightly I touched her, moving the hair back over her shoulders. "Soon it will be over," I said. "It will stop forever."

"Will it?" she said. "After thousands of years of it?"

"Yes," I said. Then I told her, as much of it as I could. "We're down here to save a man's life." And saying it made me feel an oldness, a wisdom, like someone from the Bible who has walked through sun and desert to give of his soul.

She kissed me lightly on the cheek. I put my arm around her and held her.

"If it is in one person," she said. "If goodness is in one person . . . if one person feels it inside himself. . . ."

The chill wind came whistling out of the trees. We could hear the leaves falling in the woods. I kissed her on the forehead. I thought of the woman, Rena. I had been afraid of her, not because I was mistrustful; that too, but more than that. Uncle Clay would have made love to her, and Pete Mariah had tried. But I had done nothing. What had happened later had not really altered anything. I had still been afraid of her.

I could feel Barbie's breasts against me with warm, firm pressure. My hand stroked through her hair. It was like silk, running through my fingers.

I wanted to so badly. And she was there.

But nothing happened. Even as I was releasing her I was cursing myself, saying: *Don't call yourself a man. Not yet.*

"Is it Jeffrey or Jefferson?" she asked.

"Jeffrey," I said.

"You're the kindest, most considerate person I've ever met," she said.

"Thank you," I said, not intoning the sarcasm but feeling it inside, letting it gall me, feeling it snickering at me. I stepped back, away from her. She didn't move. She just watched me, and I didn't know what that meant either. The night seemed to swell between us now. I felt my feet slipping back over the grass. I didn't know. I would never know. But I had not even tried.

I walked over to Pete. He was sitting on a rock, clicking his cold pipe between his teeth.

"So?" he said.

"So what?" I asked curtly.

"Nothing," he said. "I asked because I was sitting with my eyes closed."

"Well, you'd better open them. That Sleavey had a nose that could smell horses a mile away."

But the night passed. When there are dangers it seems that it will never pass. But it always does, lifting finally, like something that has laid unsuccessful seige, fading off in disappointment. I didn't awake until about a half-hour after sunup. When I looked up I saw her face. Then I felt her arms. She was holding me and my head was in her lap, and in this manner I had slept the soundest sleep since leaving home. She was smiling down at me. Sleep was gone but it was as if the dream had just begun. Now I saw her in daylight and she was very beautiful, the sadness still in her eyes, and my head was in her lap and her arms were around me but yet she was the dependent one. She had guarded and comforted my sleep because she was dependent.

The sky was clear and cloudless over her head. The morning was fresh and chilled. The birds had begun too, all through the woods. Her face came down, her hair sliding forward over my face like a warm curtain and her lips pressed lightly on mine for a moment and then went away.

"Good morning," she said.

When I sat up I felt a stiffness that crackled through my body. I sat and rubbed my eyes. We were at the edge of a field, surrounded on three sides by trees, on the other by the road.

"Did you sleep at all?" I asked her.

"A little."

Pete was with the horses, just inside the trees. I got up and went over to him.

"Now we've got a new problem," he said.

"What's that?"

"It ain't really none of my business," he said.

"Say it."

He was running his hand across Mark's back.

"My experience as an observer of the passing scene," he said, "tells me she won't want to leave us. Or, more precisely, you."

"That's crazy. She's got a home down here, and parents."

He shrugged. "All right, Deacon," he said.

"Just because we did her a favor. That doesn't mean anything. She's probably aching to get back. She's had a terrible experience. Why would she want to stay with us anyway?" But I was talking for my own sake. He knew that. He knew my heart was burning for her. "We'll just dump her off at her farm and that's that," I said.

"That's right," he said.

"She said it's only ten miles from here."

"She told me last night, after you had winked off, that it was just ten miles yes, but she didn't know which ten miles. She said that those two fellows had taken her through woods and around and about and that she'd lost her way."

"We'll ask directions."

"To where?"

"Mardersville."

"No such place, Deacon. She told me that too. She said the place really don't have a name, that it's just a dusty crossroads in the middle of nowhere, and that she said Mardersville because she had to give it some name."

"But we can't take her along. We've got to make time. This is no picnic we're on. Especially with those two sons of bitches still around somewhere."

"Look, Deacon," he said turning to me. "It's all right with me. You can take her along. Charl is a big strong animal; and when he gets tired she can ride as second mate on Mark."

"But it's not right, Pete," I said, trying as fast as I could to exhaust every argument against it so we could get on with it.

"She don't want to go back. She hates her Pa. Her Ma ain't her Ma but some wench her Pa's taken up with. Her real Ma is dead."

I looked at her. She was standing off near the road, watching us shyly. She knew what we were talking about. I turned back to Pete. "Well, we can't just leave her," I said.

Pete smiled. He poked me in the chest with his finger.

"How does it feel?" he asked. "Or has somebody else besides your kin ever loved you before?"

Love. First war and death and now love. Something that comes from nowhere, from inside; the one big, important contribution that people made to the world. Everything else —food and water and homes and clothing—came from the earth, from nature. But people made love. Out of the darkness, out of loneliness and despair and fortitude, people made love. Then it was there, calm and astounding, unveiled in reigning beauty, born mature and complete and self-sufficient. The one thing that equated man with his universe, with his towering mountains and his ocean masses.

How did it feel? It felt like morning, just the way morning feels when you wake up and walk in the fields and listen to the birds and feel the wind bringing on the new day.

So she rode behind me, holding me round with her arms. I'd told her once, feebly, that she had ought to go back to her Pa, but she said no. She would never go back, she said, because she had found that even in a world at war there could be kindness and compassion. She would never go back to the other kind of life. And that was that.

It was crazy, and probably wrong as well, but I didn't care. It was suddenly something that I wanted very badly to do. I would take her back to Capstone and she would live in the house and do the things that first Ma and then

Rachel before she'd got sick had done, and then I would marry her. All of that in one swift thought that became like a refrain in my mind. And then it would always be morning, all day and all night and forever.

CHAPTER 10

I told her some of it, that we were looking for my uncle, but not why—just that my uncle had to come back to Capstone and save someone's life.

"Is your uncle a soldier?" she asked.

"Sort of," I said.

"Will he come back with you?"

"When I explain, of course."

"Does he live in Capstone too?"

"That's his home, but he's seldom there. When the war is over he's coming back and buy a farm. He told me the last time that he's weary of traveling."

"Can't you tell me the rest of it?"

"I would like to," I said. "But it's sort of his personal affair. I'm concerned in it only because I want to help."

After we'd ridden a little ways I saw that we were still in the same area we'd been the night before.

"We rode in circles last night," Pete said. He was riding alongside. "If anything, we probably lost some distance."

It all looked the same around us, the lonely road, the deserted farms, the weary shedding trees, the fallen leaves strewn over the road. Here and there a muddy puddle remained from yesterday's rain. I reached into my belt and handed Pete one of the pistols. I could feel Barbie tremble behind me.

"We won't use it unless we have to," I said.

"Just the sight of them . . ." she said.

"Those two fellows might still be around somewhere."

"Especially on the road," Pete said.

"You won't have to shoot them," Barbie said. "We have horses. We'll be able to ride away from them."

"Probably," I said. But I wasn't depending on that.

So Pete told her a story, because she was so nervous. He could do that sometimes with one of his outlandish stories, just make you forget everything. It was one of the stories he told from time to time, the kind that people believed sometimes because he told them with such sincerity as though he really believed them himself.

He told her about the temperature man. He'd told it to me once and had me half believing it.

"It reminds me," he began, addressing himself to Barbie, "of the fellow that used to live in Capstone. Jeff knew him well too. This fellow was probably the most amazing person who ever lived. No doctor or scientist or anybody, drunk or sober, could explain him. People used to call him the temperature man because he had a very unusual biological constitution. Whatever the temperature was, that's what his age would be. He claimed—and I was the only one he ever told this to—that his father was an Eskimo from the North Pole and his mother had been born in Ecuador right on the equator and somehow there had been an inharmonious scrambling of insides when he was born and so his age would always correspond with the temperature. He used to live in this shack up on the edge of town, where the marsh is. He was a tall, straight, good-looking man—in the winter and in the fall and sometimes in the spring, depending, of course, on the temperature. I remember one winter's day we were out hunting rabbits. It was about twenty degrees and he was moving up and down the hills and through the woods just like you'd expect a twenty-year-old would. Then it started to get dark and began getting colder and colder and suddenly he started crying for his mother. I saw then that the temperature had gone down to about nine above and he was just like any other little boy scared in the dark without his mother. I had to take him home by the hand.

"Then, after the winter, when spring started to come and the temperatures began to rise, he'd start to slow down. I'd go up to the shack in that real nifty weather and he'd be sitting there smoking a pipe. It'd get to be fifty and sixty and seventy degrees and his hair would be turning grayer and grayer and he'd just sit there and say he was too tired to move. The summer would come and sometimes it would go up to nearly a hundred and he would almost die because he couldn't take that. I've seen him age twenty years in one day. You know how people tend to get when they're ninety or a hundred years old. One summer we had the hottest spell anybody could recall. It must've been over ninety for ten straight days and he just lay in bed unable to move and every day it looked like he was going to die. Then a north-west wind came sweeping down and brought it down to seventy and he was up and about the next day with a vigor that amazed the doctor, who was not a man easily amazed.

"He'd have the same kind of trouble with a hard winter. If it ever got down to below zero he'd naturally die because it would mean he hadn't been born yet. He'd be like a five- or six-year-old, unable to do anything for himself. I'd have to come in and cook for him and tell him to wash himself and make sure he got to bed at eight o'clock. Then the next day it might be ten or twelve degrees and I'd catch him sneaking a smoke behind the woodshed, and by midafternoon it'd be maybe twenty degrees or so and he'd be drinking whiskey as brazenly as a drummer.

"This went on for more years than anyone could tell. Nobody knew how old he really was. Some people said he'd been in Capstone for nearly a hundred years, and always like that, getting old and young just as easily as a pendulum swings, shedding years and putting them right back on from day to day.

"Then finally he died. It was in the winter. It'd been a real fine winter, with the weather between twenty and thirty for about a month. I went up there one day and found him drinking whiskey. He'd made it himself and it tasted like vinegar and smelled like a goat, but he thought it was real nectar. When I left him he was singing-drunk, doing a hornpipe on the roof. That night the temperature took a dive. I woke up about three in the morning and it was so cold that my saliva had turned to ice. After I'd gone to the stove and made a fire and breathed in the hot air and melted the ice, I got dressed and ran over to him. I calculated it at about five degrees and the thought of that child up there in that shack dead-drunk was a terrifying one. When I got there he was dead, lying on the floor froze stiff with a smile on his face and empty bottles rolling around his head. The doctor said the next day that he'd drunk too much of that snake-juice for a five-year-old to be able to agreeably absorb and it had made all the springs pop right out of his heart. A few nights later it went down to under zero and people said well he would have disappeared anyway, so at least he went out like a man, even if he was only five."

Barbie laughed.

"Shouldn't laugh," Pete chided. "It's a sad story."

"And all the truth," I said.

"You have such strange people in Capstone," she said.

"Strange?" Pete guffawed. "He was one of the most normal."

2

We cooked lunch inside an abandoned farmhouse. It had been deserted for some time. The wind had blown in the door and the rooms—stripped of almost all furniture by either the departed occupants or else by other people—were filled with dust and leaves and twigs and whatever else the wind might carry in with it. There were three small rooms. Their combined furniture might have accommodated one room. There was a bedstead, a bureau with empty drawers hanging out, two broken chairs and the kitchen table. On the table was a piece of yellow paper held in place by a rock. On the paper was scrawled, in ink, the message: Gone To War.

"On which side I wonder," Pete said, putting the rock back down.

We took the drawers from the bureau and broke them up and made a fire in the stone fireplace that had stood so cold and empty for so long. Then we cooked the last of the food that Captain Morris had given us. After, Pete and I sat before the fire, watching it burn itself down. Behind us Barbie sat precariously on one of the chairs, staring quietly into the fire, repelled, I sensed, by even this small manner of destruction. When the fire had expired she closed her eyes as the moribund streams of smoke rose from the ashes.

"I'd like to cross the river by tomorrow," I said.

"We should be able to do that," Pete said.

"From the other side it shouldn't be much of a ride."

"Sure," Pete said. "In a day or so we might be riding with Clay again. I wonder what's all happened to him during the past few months."

"The war's been quiet," I said.

"That's when a fellow like him is most busiest, in between the fighting."

"Could be, for all we know."

"Sure he is," Pete said, excited, the way he always became when he talked of Uncle Clay. "Men like Clay are sometimes more important than even the generals. They're worth whole regiments sometimes."

I turned to Barbie. She opened her eyes. "Do you feel like traveling again?" I asked.

"Yes," she said.

"Maybe you'd like to rest for a little while."

"No."

So we rode again, down the road, past the trees and the abandoned farms. We saw two things before we reached the river that night. The first was a troop of Union cavalry. Fortunately we saw them before they saw us and we were able to swerve into the woods and conceal ourselves deep in the trees while the soldiers passed. There must have been close to a hundred of them, it took them several minutes to gallop by. They looked very fast and impressive flashing through the trees along the road, their guidon fluttering and even though I was hiding from them I was proud of them. After they'd all passed we went back to the road. We rode for a mile and then came to a small village. There were several rows of houses going up a little hill into the trees and a church steeple pointing over the trees. There were several high-porched stores along the street. The approach to the village was over a clattery wooden bridge that spanned a creek that tumbled in a white brawling down from a waterfall terrace. The street was still soft from the rain, and people and horses and wagons had churned it until it was quite muddy, great puddles of dark water lying about like openings in the earth.

There weren't many people about. Those whom we saw appeared bent upon their business, walking head down, giving us a single uninterested glance and going on. We dismounted in front of a store that had a sign nailed over its entrance which said: PARKER SELLS EVERYTHING. I walked in and a tall thin man in overalls appeared behind the counter like a materializing apparition.

"Good afternoon. I'm Parker," he said, as if people were of a habit of coming to this store to see him instead of to buy things.

"I'd like to buy some food items," I said, taking the

little bag of coins that Pa had given me out of my shirt.

Parker opened his hand and showed me the whole world. "Name them," he said.

But his expansiveness was inflated. He didn't have any bacon or ham or sugar. I had to settle for milk and bread and coffee and some vegetables and several pieces of fruit that looked superannuated.

"There's some sutlers the other side of the river," Parker said. "They're selling to the soldiers. Hear they've got everything, cheese and cakes and sardines and fresh ham. That is, if you're planning on crossing."

"Yes," I said. "We are. We're going to Baker Station."

"Well then," Parker said. "You want to cross at Christophers Ford. Road there takes you right into Baker Station. Of course you might not find it so easy getting over to the ford what with all the cavalry riding about."

"We saw some cavalry just outside of here."

"They're looking for the deserters."

"Deserters?"

"Two of 'em. They've been prowling these parts for three days now. Killed a farmer late last night."

"Killed him?" I asked. "For what?"

"For his wife."

"They're in this area?"

"Some of the men are tracking them now, trying to get them before the soldiers do, to make sure that justice is done."

While we were talking a group of rough-looking men came in. There were six of them. They looked as if they had done a good deal of hard traveling during the past hours. Their coats and trousers were spattered with mud, their boots scratched and spattered. They were carrying rifles. Their bearded faces were sullen. They moved wordlessly into the store, each exchanging a hard, meaningful glance with Parker. Some of them looked at me. None of them spoke, not even among themselves. Their attitude made them a single person and the person was like an atmosphere hard and decisive in the place, as weary and sullen as the end of desperation.

Parker made my package and pushed it across the counter toward me. His manner had changed, become coolly impersonal. He wanted to be rid of me as quickly as he could. I handed him the money, picked up the package and left. I looked back once, through the window, and all the men were knotted at the counter talking to Parker.

Pete and Barbie were sitting on the top step of the porch. Mark and Charl were nuzzling in the water trough.

"How did you like that bunch of aristocrats?" Pete asked.

"Men of purpose," I said, for no good reason.

I filled our haversacks with what I had bought and then we mounted and rode off again, going slowly through the mud, slowly until we were beyond the village and the road hardened again and became very narrow, the trees touching high overhead, the shadows flicking over us as we rode beneath.

"The fellow in the store said there's lots of cavalry about," I said.

"There's going to be lots of soldiers from now on," Pete said.

"As long as they're all blue," I said. I didn't say anything about Sleavey. It was something that I preferred Barbie not to have to know. But as it turned out I didn't have to say anything. Because that was the second thing we saw that afternoon. We came around a bend and there they were, Sleavey and the other one. Like sides of beef hanging from the butcher's wall, and the air around as still and tense as though a door had just slammed. The first thing I thought was how great the difference was in their sizes; Sleavey's feet being almost a foot nearer the ground than the other's. The breeze was turning them in a vague little semicircle. They looked to be asleep there, their heads bent helplessly against the heavy twists of hangman's knot.

Barbie gasped and Pete was so startled that Mark reared up for a second. Then we sat there, in that awful stillness, staring at them. I felt Barbie's face pressed against my back, could feel the empty little sobs in her throat. Pete glanced at me, his face in a grimace.

The breeze turned Sleavey upon us and we saw his tongue hanging out as though something sour were on it. His long arms hung still at his sides, his toes—his boots removed—pointing down. His pockets had been turned inside out.

"They look fresh," Pete said.

I nodded.

"The aristocrats?" Pete asked.

"Most likely," I said, the sound of my voice giving me a hollow feeling. I had, as I stared at Sleavey's grotesque posture of death, an inexplicable feeling of pity for him—for this man, this deserter and murderer, who would have robbed and perhaps even killed us if given the chance. And then I knew why I felt this. It was because of what Captain Morris had said about men being changed by war. Perhaps this had happened to Sleavey, perhaps the evils of war had crept into his blood and corrupted it and crusted the wellsprings of good and bent him differently. And because of it he had had to die like this, and to be left gaping sightlessly at a roadside where men passed without time for prayer or pity.

Then Barbie sobbed. "Jeff. Please." And we went on, slowly down the road.

3

We reached Christophers Ford about midnight. A strong, cool wind was rushing a mighty singing through the trees. The river was rolling with a constant, muffled roaring, coursing with massed power through the dark; a timeless and effortless monotony to it as though it were bound to some massive wheel. We rode parallel to it, moving through the trees, enchanted by the great sound. Soon we saw a small, red fire burning up ahead, like an eremite's heart in the black, fallen night. At the sound of our approach a soldier appeared, moving through the trees in a mass of shadows, peering at us, rifle in hand. He moved before the fire and stood in front of it like a black statue. When we rode into the firelight's realm he suddenly threw his rifle to his shoulder and leveled it upon us with a command to halt. Then another soldier, this one with an officer's markings, appeared. A placid gesture of his hand made the other lower his rifle. He was a short, well-made man. He wore a slouch hat and a long overcoat which covered him to his ankles. He came moving up out of the dark and stood where the fire threw dark tongues of shadow up and down him.

"We've got to get to Baker Station," I said, talking down over Charl's lowered patient head to the officer. I didn't know why: I mean I didn't know what reason to give. Then it occurred to me that I was going to have to give him a reason, that I had to get to Baker Station but could not do it if I did not give this man a reason, and that it would have to be a convincing one because of the way he was standing there small and compact and mistrustful, made somehow intractable and appallingly mighty by the iron flow of overcoat that hid his body and made him look like a small, impassable wall.

"Miss Barbie's mother," I said, "is unwell and suffering there. Pete and I rode up to Baltimore to fetch her. Now we've got to bring her back."

"I see," the officer said. But I couldn't tell whether he saw or not, the way he was standing there solid and uncommitted with that fire burning slow and brittle behind him. He looked at Barbie. Then at Pete. Then back to me. "When did you leave?"

"A few days back," I said. "A week or so."

"Did you cross the river at this point?"

"Yes, sir," I said, hoping it was the right thing.

"I don't recall seeing you," he said.

"I don't recall seeing you either," I said.

He nodded at that and wiped his hand slowly across his chin for a moment. Then said, "It's unwise to be traveling hereabouts just now. When you get into Baker Station you'd better stay put." Then turning to the soldier with the rifle, he said, "Take them down to Sergeant Bryan and have him take them across."

The officer stepped aside and waved us on and we followed the soldier—he remained afoot—past the fire which glowed and dilated like a savage flower and back into the unrelieved darkness. But then other fires began rising out of the night, shadowy soldiers lurking nearby, none of whom seemed able to materialize as we passed them by. The trees began to thin out around us and the ground to slope. Then we smelled the water, the full rich wind sweeping off it, and it became very loud, inundating the air with a deep, brawny noise. We could see its powerful flowing breast now in the dark, its bumping waves catching and throwing off the reddish glints of the campfires, thronging ahead on its muscular tides.

There we stopped. The soldier went ahead toward a fire where another soldier was sitting gazing into the flames, then looking up startled at the other's approach. They spoke for a moment and then the sitting one suddenly leaped up, as he did casting aside with absolutely uninhibited abandon an empty bottle which crashed painfully among some rocks. He flashed a perfunctory salute that went clear over his head and went striding vigorously toward a horse tethered nearby.

The first soldier came back.

"The sergeant is a trifle ill," he said. "But he'll take you across." Then, with a pained backward glance, he went back.

I had sat around the porches of Capstone enough times to be able to make a swift and accurate diagnosis of the sergeant's illness, particularly when he rode up close enough for me to whiff his breath.

"The lieutenant says to take you-all across," he said, his

voice loaded with official gravity. He saluted, this time knocking his hat askew. Then he whirled his horse and rode up onto the bridge and we followed, our horses clattering importantly on the boards. Suddenly it became a race as the sergeant swept his hat from his head and wheeled it around through the air, then thrusting his body stiffly forward he emitted an exultant yell to charge and his horse did a stiff little dance and then went flying across the bridge; and we were following, racing with a sudden reckless speed that amazed and exhilarated me; chasing the sergeant who continued his spirited shouting. After crossing, we found the sergeant waiting for us, sitting his horse, panting and grinning.

"Mission achieved!" he bellowed, saluting crisply, this time with a successful regulation snap. "Welcome to Virginia."

"Which way to Baker Station?" I asked.

He waved toward a road that waited mysteriously in the night. "Follow her straight on," he said, beginning to move with his restless horse. Suddenly he threw it forward into full gallop and went pouring back into the night. We could hear him as he returned across the bridge, shouting commands to whatever ghost battalions were marching in the night.

We sat in stunned silence until we stopped hearing him. Then Pete said, "That's the brightest side of sober I've seen in a long time."

We encountered several groups of mounted soldiers during the night and to each we told the same story we had told the officer at the bridge. It seems that with a lie the hardest part is telling it the first time; after that it becomes easy and people believe it easier too. Once we even had some troopers guide us along a part of the road that forked and was not easy to follow. Pete even said that if it weren't for Barbie we probably would not have got through.

"A pretty face can be a lethal weapon if it knows how to bat its eyelashes," Pete said.

We rested for a few hours that night and reached Baker Station in the morning. It was a disappointment, as I suppose any place less than Richmond would have been after the long journey. The buildings were drab clapboard, standing in uneven rows upon the streets, looking as if they had been built by sullen men and then rejected. There was a courthouse and several brick buildings in the center of town. The flagpole atop the courthouse flew no colors, pointing straight and barren toward the gray sky. There were some elegant private homes along the wooded outskirts of the town, but these were boarded up, left behind by their flown occupants.

We rode down the little hill which led into the town. Riding down I saw the place. It was a large gray, frame building, one of the largest structures in town, three-storied, with many windows. In black letters that stretched across its length it read: BLACKHURST'S.

"There it is," I said, moving Charl more briskly. We rode around to the rear of the building. It was still early morning and no one was about. We rode into the yard and I dismounted, leaving Barbie sitting Charl by herself, and strode across the yard to the stable. I pulled open the door. The horse smell floated out, warm and heavy in the cool morning air. I walked to the first stall and looked in and saw Uncle Clay's sorrel sprawled on the straw, the same horse I had ridden up to the jail that night last summer. I went out, closing the door.

"He's here," I said. "You two stay here. I'm going inside to find him."

Pete said, "Here." He was handing me the other pistol. I reached up and took it and then went around the side of the building and then up the steps, across the porch. One door led into the tavern, the other into the lobby where the desk was; the tavern was empty so I chose the latter door. There was a man behind the desk, sitting down. I could see just his bald head. He was in a rocker, apparently, and his head kept moving back and forth. He started to look at me as I walked toward him but I never had a chance to talk to him because someone was coming down the stairs. I heard the person first, then saw his boots which looked like they were dancing, and then the rest of him. I recognized him immediately, even though I had never seen him with a beard before. Halfway down he stopped and put his hand on the rail.

"Jeffrey," he said.

"Clay."

He came down now, slowly, watching me. He came toward me, tall and wary and tired-seeming, and now his face started to look different in the beard, his eyes different, his head held up, looking down at me. His clothing was creased and dirty, his trousers tucked into his boots.

"Jeffrey," he said again.

"I have to see you," I said. "It's very important. I came all this way."

"How important can it be?" he said. He looked at the

clerk behind the desk, who was watching us now, telling the clerk something with his eyes as he put his arm around my shoulder. He led me through the door and into the tavern. It was damp and chilly in there, looking strange in its emptiness, like something stricken immobile in the midst of buoyant animation.

We sat at a table. Uncle Clay sat back, his shoulders squared against the back of the chair, his hands dropped in his lap.

"So, Jeff," he said. I just stared at him for a moment. He was different. He was heavier, for one thing, and the beard changed him completely, made him older.

"It's about Pa, and Rachel."

"What about them?"

"Rachel's in a way. Pa thinks George Adamson did it and is going to take after him with the shotgun."

"I see," he said. He took into account right away that I knew, he covered that gap right away. "And you want me to come back and 'fess up." He smiled. Even through the beard the smile was still warm and disarming, except that now the beard gave it an odd, sarcastic look. "Well, you know I'm doing important work down here."

"But it's Pa. . . ."

"Yes, Jeff, I know. Does he know who you came down here after?"

"I don't think so."

"He's going to wait for you to get back?"

"Yes."

"And Rachel?"

"She won't tell."

"You place me in a very difficult position, Jeff," he said, still sitting there with his shoulders back against the chair, his hands in his lap, very calm about it, as though it were not so difficult at all. "On the one hand there's my duty here, and on the other your Pa. But of course I'll go back."

I could feel all the misgivings melting, a warm elation beginning to spiral.

"I'll be your uncle and brother-in-law both at the same time," he said with a laugh.

"We brought your pistols," I said taking them out and putting them on the table.

His eyes appraised them warmly. "Good. I don't have that old iron you gave me in Capstone, but you can have this one that I've been using." He pulled a pistol from his holster which was concealed under his coat and gave it to me. Then he asked, as if he had just heard it, " 'We?' "

"Pete Mariah. He came along."

"Pete? Well, I should have known. Where is he?"

"He's outside with the horses, and the girl."

"Girl? What girl?"

"Barbie. We found her. Saved her from two deserters. She wants to come back to Capstone with us."

"Well, Jeff," he said with a smile.

"It's not like that," I said, my face blushing.

"Of course not. Well, let's go see them." He stood up. "By the way, how did you think of coming here?"

"Alamine Johnson told me."

"Oh," he said. "And what led you to him?"

"Judge Stetterson."

"The Judge, eh? And how is he?"

"He's very well."

"I'm glad for that," he said, with some irony, I thought.

As we walked toward a rear door he put his arm around my shoulders and said, "Look, Jeff, there's going to be some trouble around here shortly and I don't want you getting caught up in it. I'll have to stay an extra day or so, but you and the others can ride out this afternoon and get back into Maryland. I'll join you up north somewhere."

"I'd rather wait for you."

"It will be better the other way."

"But—"

"You do as I say."

Pete and Barbie were sitting on a bench in the yard. Pete jumped up and ran toward Uncle Clay and they shook hands and Uncle Clay clapped him on the shoulder. Then Uncle Clay went to Barbie. He made a courtly greeting, bowing slightly from the waist. I saw she was afraid of him, didn't like him. I had that feeling and it was very strange. I had never seen a stranger—a woman particularly—ever react like that to him before. They were always charmed and flattered. But she just smiled thinly and stared back at him.

"Jeff tells me you're coming back with us to Capstone," he said, his voice low and quiet, almost murmurous, the way he could make it sometimes, the way he always spoke to Rachel, the kind of voice that could make you sleepy if you listened long enough to it.

"Yes," she said. "Jeff is very kind."

"We try to make that a family trait," Uncle Clay said.

"Jeff succeeds," she said.

Then Pete jumped in. "Tell us about that night, Clay," he said.

"Which night is that, Pete?" Uncle Clay said, turning to him, smiling in the beard.

"You know—when we brought you the horse and the pistol."

He clapped Pete on the shoulder again. "Well, we'll do a lot of talking after you people have had a good, hot meal and perhaps bathed and had a change of clothing. Let's go inside."

We had the hot meal, and the baths, and Uncle Clay got us a change of clothing—for the three of us—from where I don't know. But he had that knack of doing things. We ate in his room on a long table that was carried in and elegantly spread with real silverware. We didn't care that it was only about nine o'clock in the morning as we went through a meal that was breakfast, lunch and supper all in one, gulping down one course after another almost as fast as we could smell them.

Uncle Clay didn't eat. He sat back and enjoyed himself watching us, slapping his leg with a riding crop. Several times someone knocked on the door and Uncle Clay had to go out. There were whispered conversations in the hall and then he came back smiling.

"I won't be divulging any secrets, I don't think," he said, "if I told you that there's going to be some heat in the air around here very shortly. So I want you three to get out as soon as you can. I'll join up with you later."

"Where?" I asked.

"Well, let's see," he said frowning. He opened his blouse

and pulled a well-worn map out and opened it upon the table, holding down one corner of it with his thumb. "Here," he said, pointing as I peered over his shoulder. "Weemsboro. It's a little town. Not much there, except that I have some friends there, people who run a place sort of like Blackhurst's, an inn and tavern. They'll probably be there when you arrive. Ask for Matthew. Tell him who you are. . . ."

He went on, said more, but I wasn't listening. Pete was looking at me. We tried to say too many things with our eyes, explanations and reasons and suspicions, and should we tell Uncle Clay about his friends in Weemsboro; and Pete left it to me, and I said nothing.

"Do you have it?" Uncle Clay was asking, looking up over his shoulder at me.

"Yes," I said, looking at him. "I have it."

"I'll be there in two days at the most."

"Suppose you're not there by then?"

"Well, Jeff, this is war and nothing is ever certain in war." Then he dropped that uncharacteristic tone and smiled. "But I'll be there."

4

We left that afternoon. It was gray and chilly, the rain up in the sky but not fallen yet. Uncle Clay stood at the foot of the porch steps watching us mount. He had got a horse for Barbie, where, I don't know, it was one of those things that he could do, and did. He helped her to mount and then stood back.

"Be careful," he said.

"Yes," I said. "It's become our habit." I didn't look at him. I was looking at the ground.

"You know, Jeff," he said, "you're going to be shaving pretty soon."

I felt my chin. "Yes," I said.

"See you at Weemsboro," he said, slapping Charl who began to move out.

"Good-by, Clay," Pete said.

"Good-by, Pete," Uncle Clay said. "Barbie—you take care of them."

"Good-by," she said.

We rode through the town, past the few people who were on the streets now, past the courthouse and its flagless pole and on up the hill, a few fleet drops of rain in our faces.

We rode silently. Pete was watching me. I could feel his eyes on me, waiting for me to say something. But we didn't have to say anything. We were both thinking the same. And before we could say or do anything we were going to have to ride. There was nothing else for us to do but ride, as if we were going to have to run away from ourselves before we could pull up and look at each other and start to talk. Because it wasn't that easy. It was simple and obvious and uncomplicated, but it still wasn't easy, because we both loved him and he was always our god and it was as if someone had just said that all gods must die and we didn't want to believe it.

But in a moment we didn't have the chance even to think about it. Riding outside of town, on the road toward the ford, we suddenly saw several Union cavalrymen. They were galloping pell-mell down the road. They galloped to a halt when they came to us. One, a major, glared at us.

"What are you doing here? Get off this road!" he cried.

"Why?" I asked.

"Never mind why—just get to hell off of the road!"

Then we saw why. Coming down the road were more horses and more moving things than I had ever seen in my life—horses and mules and wagons and ambulances and batteries of artillery, and marching alongside, at the sides of the road, long blue columns.

The major galloped on. Another officer shouted to us as he moved to follow, "They'll ride right over you! Get off!"

We turned into the woods, picking our way through the trees as fast as we could. Then we paused to watch them. We could see them passing, an endless train of men and horses and wagons and cannon, rattling and thundering. Mounted officers swirled in and out shouting orders. Groups of cavalry came pounding by at steady intervals, forcing the soldiers into the woods.

"There's going to be some battle," Pete whispered reverently.

"Clay said it," I said dryly.

More and more caissons came thundering by, followed by more wagons which bumped and rattled over the rugged road, and then more cannon. Then long columns of soldiers with flags flying, rifles shouldered, marching in steady, unbroken, inexorable file.

"We're going to have a hell of a time getting over that bridge," I said. "We'll have to find another road."

But I didn't move. Something kept me fixed there, watching them, watching the dust float up over the flags in thin, yellow clouds. I began to sense a deep, sad brooding somewhere far in my soul. It felt uneasy because it was strange. It was no mere stirring, but something building, creating some strong edifice of emotion. And then, as though someone had touched a wand to an unflowered stem and made it bloom in a hot vivid flowering, I knew. I was proud. Proud of these soldiers, of the clamor and the excitement, of the illusory glory they presented. It was as if I were gazing upon some already achieved historical thing, the glorious flowing motion of some heroic mural. But it was no mural, no illusion, and the glory would be soiled with blood and wreckage; these men were marching now, before my eyes; marching aware and alert down a road they knew was pronged with death. Marching to fight for me, for Pa and Rachel and Tom.

The mad desire to race and join them seized me. It was like a fit of inspiration, making my brain blaze and my heart race. To suddenly participate, to enter the selfless flow of columns and cast my arms with them. As far as my eye could travel I could see them, coming and coming and coming. I remembered the things Captain Morris had said, and now they seemed—his words—to have become embodied in the columns of soldiers. My heart ached with love and loyalty and terror.

Then Pete said, "Deacon. We ought to move out."

"Yes," I murmured. The vision had passed before my eyes and was now entering my heart. Reluctantly I turned Charl and began to ride.

We rode on through the woods, getting farther and farther away from the Army. Charl breasted aside the branches and the bushes with a great powerful slowness.

After about a half-hour we struck another road. It was little more than a path through the woods. We followed it, moving at a gallop. Crossing a stream we came through the trees and suddenly upon four men kneeling on the ground reading a map. At our appearance they leaped up and we found ourselves faced with drawn pistols.

"What's this?" one asked.

"It's too bad for them, that's what," another said.

They were wearing Confederate uniforms, none of them marked by rank. Their bearded faces were partially covered by slouch hats.

I felt an angry helplessness, as if someone had pinned my arms. My pistol lay tucked into my belt, under my coat. But it felt like something that was asleep there, of no utter use to me. So there was nothing I could do, nothing I could say.

"No, it's not bad for them," one of them said, moving to the front, putting his pistol into his belt. I recognized the pistol before I did the man. He stood tall and erect, unashamed, proud, even arrogant, pushing his hat slowly up from his face.

"Well, Jeff," he said. "So now you know."

"Who is it? Who are they?" one of the men asked, his voice fast and anxious, like a blind man's.

Uncle Clay silenced him with a raised hand.

"We got lost," I said. "There's soldiers all over the road." I looked at him. He could see it in my eyes, the contempt, the hate.

"This is not very good, Jeff," he said.

"I ought to be saying that to you," I said.

"Who the *hell* is it?" the anxious one asked again, restive.

Uncle Clay turned on them. "Mount up," he said, ordered. "Gather up the map and mount up. I'll meet you in ten minutes at the mill." They looked back at him. Now his voice changed, became like steel, like an invisible saber slashing at them. "Out!" he cried. "Get out!"

Wordlessly they went, mounting and riding off up the road. He watched them until they had disappeared through the trees. Then he turned around, his eyes rising to meet mine.

"There isn't time for explanations, Jeff," he said. "You've seen what you've seen, and that's all there is to it."

"Then they were right," I said, saying it more to myself.

"Yes, they were right. But there isn't time to explain."

"Then you're not coming back?"

"No."

"Not even if Pa. . . ."

"There isn't time, Jeff," he said tersely. "Now turn around and get out of here. You have your life. What more do you want? This road will get you out of here. Follow it due north. You'll reach a ford. . . ."

"And what of Pa, and Rachel?" I said.

"And what of the thousands that are going to die in a few days?" he said impatiently.

"Yes," I said. "Thousands of soldiers. . . ."

His eyes flared angrily. "What does that matter to you?"

"It does," I said stubbornly. "It matters a lot."

"Well, it shouldn't. Really, Jeff, it doesn't make much difference who wins. For people like you and me things will hardly change."

"That's not true," I said, still stubborn, as if my argument could still influence him.

He went toward his horse. We watched him mount.

"Go home, Jeff," he said.

"And when people ask. . . ."

"Tell them some story. You're a clever lad. When it's all over I'll come back and explain. But now there isn't time."

He started to turn, to ride off. I called his name, but he didn't stop. He wouldn't stop. I must have been opening my coat and reaching my hand in even as I was talking to him because I heard Barbie scream. That made him turn in his saddle. So it wasn't in the back. He saw the pistol he had just given me in my hand and his eyes dilated not with fear or surprise but rage, with a rage that was a more incisive comment than any words could have made.

I fired once and his hand flew against his breast and he tumbled out of the saddle as his horse bolted. He hit the ground hard and lay there, the blood immediate out of his chest, his hat rolled away, one leg drawing slowly up.

Barbie screamed again. She came alongside me, her face livid, her eyes furious. *"Beast!"* she shrieked. *"Animal!"* I looked emptily at her as she whipped her horse and tore off into the woods.

Then the shock left me. "Get her, Pete!" I yelled. He took off after her as I leaped down and ran to Uncle Clay. As I ran I heard the crash in the woods and saw Pete and Mark going down, hearing Pete's abrupt yell. I looked at Uncle Clay. His eyes were open but they were like the eyes of the Confederate soldier we had watched die; the dreamy fury frozen in them, glazed over and sealed by a soft, ineffable film. Dust particles mingled in the stream of blood that ran down his breast and crawled along the road.

Then I ran to Pete. Mark was just getting up, turning bewilderedly in the trees. Pete was rolled over, half in the stream, looking up at me, dazed and ashamed, his eyes filled with some vague pain that his brain had not as yet located.

I looked into the woods. I couldn't see her. I couldn't hear her either any more, after a few more seconds. I ran back to my horse and was about to mount but never got farther than one foot into the stirrup. I brought it down and turned around. I looked again at Uncle Clay, then at Pete, at the water running over his legs in the stream. I went to Pete and took him under the armpits and pulled him gently from the water.

"I'm sorry, Deacon," he said with a groan.

"So am I," I said. I could feel the tears welling up in my eyes, warm little strangers, warm and sad and soft. Then I felt them rolling slowly down my cheek as I just sat there and looked at nothing.

CHAPTER 11

There was snow when we got back. We began getting it in Pennsylvania and when we reached Capstone there was a thick carpet of it, fallen upon the fields and roads, on the rooftops and in the empty trees, cold and silent everywhere. We rode up Grant Avenue through it, past the chimney-smoking stores and houses. The snow-whitened town seemed to have taken on great age during the past weeks. Or perhaps it was myself.

Only once during the long, slow trip back did we speak of Uncle Clay. That was when Pete said,

"Why? Because of your Pa and Rachel, or because of the uniform?" And I replied,

"Not because of them, no. Because of what he was doing, not what he had done."

"I never thought it could happen," Pete murmured.

"What?" I asked. "That he could die, or that I should have been the one to have done it?"

"Both," Pete said.

Of Barbie I said, "Someday, when it's over, I'll go back and find her and try to explain." But I would never do that, I knew. It was just something I had to say to try and complete it. I had thought of her hard and often after we had begun traveling north. Sometimes I would think of her more than I would of Uncle Clay. But then, during the last few days, I found I was thinking less and less of her. I had hoped that someday she would understand, but then I didn't care if she ever understood or not.

We rode past the Dooley House, past the empty porch and came to the crossroads.

"I guess your folks will be surprised," I said.

"They're too old for that," Pete said. "They'll just sigh and say, 'He's back.' "

"Well," I said.

"I'll bring Mark back tomorrow," Pete said. Then he rode off, huddling against the cold.

I rode along through the snow, cold and tired now. From the top of the hill I saw the house again, smoke floating thinly from the chimney against the bleak winter sky; and the tree, stolid and indomitable in its winter covering. And I leaned forward and whispered into Charl's perking, limber ears:

"We're home."

2

Pa said that he had known, that he had taken a good hard look at George Adamson and known that George could never have done it, and that the only other possible one had been

Uncle Clay. When he met me at the porch he snorted and said,

"I knew he wouldn't come back with you."

Later, when I told him what I had done, and why, I felt sorry that he was my father, because suddenly he was in such baffling sorrow. I watched him sink into his chair before the fire and I wished that he wasn't my father because I didn't want to see my father in such sorrow. But he said, talking low and quiet to the fire, "You did the only thing you could. I would have done the same."

Rachel was gone. Pa had taken her to a place some weeks before. They would care for her there, he said, and there she would have the baby. Perhaps someday, he said, she would be well again.

Tom made me sit up all night with him telling him the stories of what had happened. I don't think I slept two hours before I heard Pete Mariah downstairs making a racket. Pa threw him out once, calling him a horse thief, but then Pete came in through the back door and Pa gave up.

Pete and I sat before a great fire in the hearth, smoking our pipes.

"You think you had troubles before, Deacon," he said. "But now they've multiplied beyond human computation."

"How's that?" I asked.

"I told my sisters what you did. At first they grieved. They were all in love with Clay you know. But when I told them why you did it they proclaimed you a great hero and each of them has transferred their affections to you. They can be very aggressive young ladies—all five of them. They make up in determination what they lack in other things. My advice to you is to marry the first one that comes swimming through the snow. You'll never know a peaceful moment until you do."

"Which one would you recommend?" I asked.

"It makes little difference," he said. "They're all homely and none has any money, and no matter which one you take, I'm still your brother-in-law."

THE END